The only sound was the snow crunching under their feet.

Nora leaned into Rush as they walked to the cabin.

Crack!

The gunshot sprayed the snow a foot from them.

Someone had been lying in wait, Rush realized. To get her. To get them.

"Run!" When Nora obeyed his command, he ushered her behind a tree.

Another shot fired, this one splintering the bark, and he fired back. Grabbing Nora's hand, he hauled her into the woods with him.

When they'd made it deep inside, the firing stopped.

"Now what do we do?" Nora asked, her panting breath coming out in plumes in the cold night.

Either the shooter had given up...or he was tracking them quietly. Stalking them.

"We double back to the chalet and call for backup," he told her.

But his deputy sheriff's mind reeled with the potential danger. With a list of potential suspects. Someone had planned this attack carefully. Could be anyone. Nora's mother had had a slew of deadly secrets...

And now one of them was out to get Nora.

Jessica R. Patch lives in the mid-South, where she pens inspirational contemporary romance and romantic suspense novels. When she's not hunched over her laptop or going on adventurous trips with willing friends in the name of research, you can find her watching way too much Netflix with her family and collecting recipes for amazing dishes she'll probably never cook. To learn more about Jessica, please visit her at jessicarpatch.com.

Books by Jessica R. Patch

Love Inspired Suspense

Fatal Reunion
Protective Duty
Concealed Identity
Final Verdict
Cold Case Christmas

The Security Specialists

Deep Waters
Secret Service Setup
Dangerous Obsession

COLD CASE CHRISTMAS

JESSICA R. PATCH

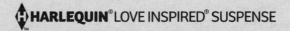
HARLEQUIN® LOVE INSPIRED® SUSPENSE

Recycling programs
for this product may
not exist in your area.

LOVE INSPIRED BOOKS

ISBN-13: 978-1-335-49080-3

Cold Case Christmas

www.Harlequin.com

Printed in U.S.A.

The name of the Lord is a strong tower:
the righteous runneth into it, and is safe.
–Proverbs 18:10

To the lonely and fearful hearts. God sees. He knows.
He loves you and is always for you. Stand firm
in your faith and trust He's working on your behalf.
Perfect love casts out all fear.

As always, thank you to...

my brainstorming partner and rough draft reader,
Susan Tuttle; my wonderful agent, Rachel Kent;
and my brilliant editor, Shana Asaro. It takes a village
to birth a book. Thank you for being my village!

Special thanks to: Michael Fagin at West Coast Weather
for helping me with the forensic meteorology portion
of the story. Any mistakes or stretches I made for
fictional purposes are all on me! You were wonderful
to talk to and provided a plethora of information.
I appreciate your time in answering all of my questions
thoroughly and professionally.

ONE

A country a version of "Holly Jolly Christmas" played inside Chief Deputy Sheriff Rush Buchanan's Bronco. His coffee steamed from the insulated thermos and sleet pelted his windshield. Blue lights flashed and cast eerie shadows over Shepherd Rock Lake. Wind jostled his vehicle as he slid his hands into his lambskin gloves. Nothing about this moment was "holly" or "jolly."

He opened the door and braved the nasty weather. East Tennessee had its perks, though. Splendor Pines was the gateway to the gorgeous Smoky Mountains, capped in white at the moment. But now, in the darkness, with the mountains shadowing the horizon, everything appeared sinister, especially with the headlights shining on the rusted and mud-caked car they'd dragged from the lake.

The crunching of tires on gravel turned Rush's attention from the car and the pit in his gut. Sherriff Troy Parsons parked beside him and climbed out. He frowned and flipped his collar over his ears. "Well?" he asked in his gruff voice.

"It's a Jaguar. Deputy Tate ran the plates. It's hers."

Troy grunted. Rush didn't need to expound. Marilyn Livingstone had driven a Jaguar and she'd been missing since Christmas Eve seventeen years ago.

"Remains inside?"

"Skeletal. I think DNA is going to confirm it."

"Any other remains?"

"No."

Troy cocked his head, studied the vehicle dripping with water and debris. "Theories?"

Rush had plenty. But speculating aloud wasn't smart. Especially with the small crowd that had gathered. He moved closer to Troy, his mentor and father figure after Dad became a shell of the man he once was. "I know rumors say she ran off with a man that Christmas Eve." One of many she'd been whispered to have had affairs with. Not all were lies. Rush had witnessed it with his own eyes on the very night Marilyn vanished. Only Troy knew his secret.

Troy hunched in the cold and rolled his toothpick around lips that were hidden by a dark mustache and beard. "You want to call the Livingstones? Or would you rather not deal with talking to the eldest daughter?"

"You can say her name." Nora. The woman Rush thought he was going to marry. Then Marilyn went missing and metaphorically, so did Nora. She retreated into herself and broke things off just before she left for college. Rush sighed, took his flashlight and trudged through the snow to the car. A crime scene tech was photographing and collecting materials. "Find anything?"

"A round, silver cuff link and partial remains of a man's masquerade mask."

Could they have belonged to the man Rush had seen Marilyn with that night? He turned to Troy. "How do you want to proceed?"

"I don't know why she'd be out this far from home with the biggest event of the year going on, but it turned into a tragic accident. Pretty cut-and-dried, don't you think?"

Seemed so. "Suppose we'll know more once Gary can examine the bones. Course he won't be able to determine cause of death if it's drowning," Rush said.

"What else would it be? Other than maybe the impact of crashing into the lake knocked her out. I'll be honest, I hope that's the case and she wasn't conscious when the waters took her. But let's leave it to Gary. He ought to be rolling in soon."

Rush agreed.

"We need to call Joshua," Troy said. "He'll want to know we've discovered his wife." Joshua Livingstone owned the biggest resort and lodge in Splendor Pines. A powerful man, but one of the kindest Rush had ever known. He'd handled the many rumors about his wife with poised grace. Which—if Rush hadn't witnessed Marilyn kissing a man in a Phantom of the Opera mask that night of the annual Christmas Eve Masquerade Ball—he wouldn't have believed. What kind of man wouldn't have a meltdown over his wife cheating on him? Numerous times—if all the tales were true.

Rush adjusted his wool collar; icy beads had steadily slicked down his neck, but he didn't mind. His whole body was flushed. "I guess Nora will come home." Granted she came every Christmas Day, but only for the day. Rush had to share some of the blame for that.

"You ready?" Troy asked.

Was anyone ready to see the person they thought they'd have the rest of their lives with? "I've moved on, Troy."

"And your last date was?"

"Six months ago with Brandy Walker." She was sweet. Lived in the neighboring town. They met at a church singles social. But he hadn't felt a spark. Would he ever? Would he always be a lonely bachelor living in a house too big for one man on the side of the mountain?

Troy grunted. "I know Nora was a pretty little thing. Still is. But at some point, you're going to have to stop comparing other women to her. Who's to say you'd even have a thing in common with her anymore?"

The downside to father figures. They felt the license to say whatever and whenever. And however. "I'm over Nora Livingstone. Not finding the right woman has nothing to do with her and everything with God's timing." Which was slower than Grandma Buchanan's homemade sorghum. "Sometimes I wish you weren't my mentor," he deadpanned.

"Sometimes I do too." Troy smirked. "I'll call Joshua and give him the news. Merry early Christmas."

"And a happy New Year to no one," Rush muttered.

Troy shook his head and climbed back inside his vehicle to make the call, leaving Rush to the wreckage. The body. *Why would you leave Nora and Hailey, Marilyn?* She may not have been faithful to her husband, but she'd doted on her girls.

New gawkers arrived with local media.

"Is that Marilyn's car?" a few asked.

"Poor Joshua."

"He's probably relieved to be rid of that…"

Insults, opinions and gossipy speculation rode on the wind, slapping Rush's face with frozen fingers. Gossip murdered the spirit. He'd witnessed it happen to his own father. Over ten years now and he'd never returned to pastoring or part-time law enforcement no matter how hard Rush and the rest of his family prayed. Dad had chosen to hide from everything and everyone.

Rush turned on the crowd. "Someone is dead. This

person had family and friends, so show a little respect, please, or I'll have every last one of you dragged from here. Am I clear?"

The onlookers quieted. For now.

Before long a black Escalade pulled up next to Rush's Bronco. Joshua Livingstone—larger than life in his long, black fancy coat—stepped out. Jet-black hair and intense eyes, the same color, focused on Rush. "Troy called." His voice was baritone but soft. Rush recognized the sorrow, the need for answers. Hailey, Nora's younger sister, sat in the passenger side, tears rolling down her cheeks—she looked so much like her sister, only her hair was a darker blond and she had Joshua's eyes. She'd been through a lot lately with her separation from her husband. She and their son lived at the main house with Joshua. Rush hated to be the bearer of bad news, but now they might be able to find peace.

"All we know is the car is registered to you, and I'm sure you can tell it's Marilyn's. The...remains need a DNA test but I'm pretty sure they'll come back as your wife's. I'm so sorry for your loss, Joshua."

Troy returned and shook hands with Joshua.

Joshua stared at the car. "Any idea what happened?"

Rush sighed and glanced at the car that had once been shiny and sleek. "You know what the weather is like up here this time of year. Seems a tragic accident."

Joshua nodded. "When can we have her for a proper burial?"

"We need to officially confirm it's her. After that, I see no reason why you can't have her back."

They stood silently staring for several long minutes until another set of headlights flashed behind Joshua's Escalade. Rush squinted, blinded by the lights. The driver didn't bother to kill them before the door to the car opened and a woman's figure stepped out, slipped under the crime scene tape and stomped toward him.

"Hey," he shouted. "You can't be out here."

"The cumulus clouds I can't!" she hollered back.

Rush wouldn't freeze from the nearly single-digit temps. But his heart froze at the sound of Nora's voice. Sassy. Southern—though a little less country in it than he remembered, but then she'd moved to Knoxville and taken a prestigious job as Chief Meteorologist. He watched her every night at six online. Didn't much care about the weather unless it affected his townspeople. He watched to see her sunshiny smile with a chance of twinkle in her blue-green eyes.

Right now, she was all storm clouds and thunder. But even so she was a sight to behold, dressed in a soft but thick coat, gray beanie and knee-high leather boots. He couldn't seem to find his voice.

Nora marched up to him, as if the weather didn't bother her in the least. She nearly reached his chin flat-footed. The smell of cherry blossoms and vanilla filled his nose, and the familiar scent brought a wave of memories. He'd been crazy about her since third grade. But he'd gained the courage in eighth grade and asked her to a dance. They'd dated all through high school.

"Don't just stare at me, Rush. Answer me."

What had she said? "Repeat the question, please."

"Is it my mom?" She looked to her father, but he stood stoically.

Rush shook out of the memories. "DNA will confirm it, but I think it's safe to say it's your mama." Did he hug her? He wasn't sure what to do. "I'm sorry, Nora Beth," he murmured.

Nora's chin quivered and for a millisecond Rush thought she was going to fall into him. And that'd be okay. But she turned at the last second and ran into her father's arms. Looked to him for solace.

Joshua kissed Nora's cheek. "It's going to be okay, honey." She shuddered against her father's chest, then gained resolve and faced Rush.

"Do you know what happened?" she asked lightly.

"We don't, but it's dark and we haven't had a chance to thoroughly examine everything."

"You will, won't you, Rush?" She sniffed and wiped a tear.

Rush closed the gap between them and grasped her gloved hand with his. She never wanted to believe Marilyn had abandoned her family. But, here in the lake leading out of town, it appeared that was exactly what she'd done. Rush didn't know how to spare her that pain. He'd tried to spare her then by never revealing what he saw that night with Marilyn and the Phantom. But now? The evidence was right in front of her eyes.

Troy gripped her shoulder in a fatherly manner. "The roads were bad that night. Probably hit a patch of black ice. The only thing left is to confirm it is your mama and put her and this to rest, hon."

Nora gaped and freed her hand from Rush's. "Unacceptable."

"Nora," Joshua said calmly.

She shrugged him off. "Doesn't anyone want to know why she was out here? On Christmas Eve night?"

"Of course we do, but that's not relevant or even possible to know now," Troy offered.

Nora pointed with her black glove toward the car. "I know what you're thinking. The whole town has thought it for years." Her voice rose with each word. The crowd attentively listened, reporters salivated. "She wasn't leaving us. She was out here that night for a reason, and I'm going to find out if I have to turn over every rock, crawl into every hole and re-create every weather pattern for a week leading up to the event. My mother didn't leave me!" Her watery eyes met Rush's. "She didn't."

Rush itched to comfort her, but she'd push him away. The last time she left his arms, she'd called him a cheater, a liar and a jerk. He'd own up to two out of three. He didn't embrace her but he did pull her aside. "What if you don't like where that night takes you, Nora?" he asked softly. "Let it go. Be content with the fact that she loved you."

If Nora dug, it could turn up a lot of dirt.

"I will not be content until I know what she was doing out here. And just because you assume it's an accident doesn't mean it was." Nora shivered. "What if someone hurt her?"

He couldn't rule out foul play yet, but it was unlikely—even with the evidence retrieved from Marilyn's car. Nora wanted any answer other than the one that claimed her mother was leaving town without so much as a goodbye. And they'd never know the reason. It had been nearly two decades. "I told you I'd look into it, Nora."

"You promise?"

"Nora, I've never broken a promise to you. I won't break one now." He hadn't broken the promise to be together forever. She had. He'd tried everything to coax her back into the land of the living—back to him. In the end, she'd left him picking up the shattered pieces of his heart.

Her lips soured. "No, I suppose you haven't broken a promise to *me*. But you have broken them."

She hit him square in the frozen heart, thawing it to a burning muscle that pulsed with regret. He hadn't broken a promise, but he had broken a commitment to the girl he was dating when Nora came home after graduating college for a job opportunity with a radio station. He hadn't expected that, or for her to call him and see if they could grab dinner, catch up, since she'd pulled away from him after her mom went missing.

It was as if nothing had ever come between them, and she'd been planning on moving back if things went well with her interview.

Things escalated, snowballed. He honestly meant to tell Nora about Ainsley, and that he'd already intended to break things off with her anyway—it was the truth. But before he had the chance, Ainsley caught him and Nora in a heated kiss on Lookout Tower.

Angry words had been hurled. Words like *You're just like your mother. A home-wrecker.* Statements like *Wait until the town hears that perfect Nora Livingstone is her mother made over.* Nora wouldn't let Rush explain, and really what could he say? He had cheated on Ainsley with Nora. He was wrong. He admitted it. He'd made amends with Ainsley since, and she was now married to Dan, Troy's son and Rush's good friend. Water under the bridge, but Nora had tucked tail and run to Knoxville, never looked back. Never answered a call from Rush.

He glanced at Troy and ignored his disdain over Rush's declaration to look into things. It might be a waste of time and manpower, but he'd oblige Nora this one thing.

He owed her.

Nora's heart might explode. There were so many emotions going on right now. She'd come home twelve days before Christmas—not by choice—only to arrive at the lodge and be told that Dad and Hailey were out at Shepherd Rock Lake with the police. That alone sent knives to her gut. But now here she was face-to-face with Rush. Time had filled out the young man's body into a grown man's, muscled by hard outdoor work more than gym visits; she'd heard he'd built a log cabin up farther on the mountain.

His hat covered his toasted blond hair, but eyes the color of Hershey bars drilled into hers. Rush wasn't a promise breaker. He used to be the most noble and honest person she'd ever known. And he could make her laugh on a dime. But then he had hurt her and at the moment she wasn't sure he'd give the investigation all he had. Troy Parsons wanted to end it right now.

But Mom was here for a reason and Nora couldn't let it rest. However, arguing about it when she was standing in the middle of a monster Christmas storm coming through wasn't wise. She'd predicted back in September low pressures off the Gulf Coast and arctic outbreaks across the Southeast. Snowflakes had begun in early October. This was likely to be the worst snow and ice storm in twenty-five years, but she couldn't afford to fly south for the winter. She was upside down in debt and she'd been pushed out of her Chief Meteorologist job at channel six in Knoxville.

To say she was touchy was an understatement.

Dad approached her. "I'm taking Hailey home, honey. Don't stay here any longer than you feel you have to. I'll have the guest chalet stocked for you." He kissed her forehead.

She nodded at Dad and watched him climb in his vehicle. Hailey hadn't once stepped out. Not even to acknowledge Nora was home. She didn't handle hard situations well. Neither did Nora, but someone had to be Mom's voice. Someone had to find out the truth.

Nora walked closer to Mom's car. All these years, she'd been submerged. Christmas Eve used to be Nora's favorite night. The resort and lodge was always booked with families and couples from all over the world, anticipating the renowned Christmas Eve Masquerade Ball. A glorious night decorated in red, green and gold. A nativity ice sculpture. Fountains of gold sparkling cider. Christmas music. Friends. Family. Fun.

Nora's heart ached. Her father still put on the event as if her mother hadn't gone missing that night. He had barely said a word about it. Didn't push or force the investigation. Maybe he had believed the vicious murmurs about Mom.

Well, not Nora.

"Nora." Rush's voice came softer than moss. "Don't go any closer. Some things can't be unseen."

And some things couldn't be undone. "Do you remember it raining and being slick that night?"

"I don't know," he said sadly. She glanced at him, his nose red and eyes deep with compassion and pity. If only he knew how pitiful Nora was. Not two pennies to rub together. But he'd never know. No one would. It was all too humiliating.

"I don't." Nora had always been fascinated with weather, which was why she remembered there had been snow earlier but the temps had been mild for December. "I need to trace her steps that night and find out what time she left the party and ended up here. Someone saw or heard something. They had to have." If she could piece together the weather from that fateful Christmas Eve, she might be able to determine if the car going into the lake was related to weather conditions or not. Her part-time work as a forensic meteorologist had her doing this often, helping insurance companies with claims.

Rush licked his lips and pawed his scruffy face. "Let me do it. Spend your time with family. Isn't that why you're home so early?" He cocked his head, and plumes of air trailed from his mouth.

She was here because she had nowhere else to go. When the news played and she wasn't on-screen they'd know. "I left channel six."

Rush's eyebrows rose. "Really? Why?"

The cold seeped into her bones and her teeth chattered. "I'm ready for warmer weather. Going to take a job in Florida." She hoped anyway. She ought to know in the next week or two. And right now she did want warmer weather. She was a human Popsicle.

Rush frowned. "You love mountain air. Skiing. Snowball fights."

"I do know how to pack a snowball," she quipped. "But people change. I'm ready for palm trees and waterskiing." She adjusted her knit cap and rubbed her hands, her gloves not keeping her as warm as she'd like, and stared at Mom's car. "Anything inside besides...her?"

He scratched the back of his neck. "We found a cuff link in the car, partial male masquerade mask. Haven't checked the trunk yet, but we'll gather the evidence, see what we see."

A cuff link. A mask. "A man was in the car that night?"

"Seems like." His eyes were shifty.

"What are you keeping from me?"

"Nothing pertinent to the case."

"Promise?"

"Nora, trust me."

She laughed humorlessly. "Last time I trusted you, Rush, you broke two women's hearts and made me look cheap. I'm sure the whole town thinks it." Ainsley surely spread it all over the world.

"No one thinks that, Nora, and you'd have known that if you hadn't gotten out of Dodge at world-record speed.

But that's what you do." He shoved a hand on his hip and heaved a breath.

Nora's temperature rose a few degrees. "And cheating on women. That's what you do?"

Rush's jaw ticked. "We were kids. And I was going to tell you."

"We were twenty-one. And you didn't. You gave the town a new tale to spin." But fighting about it was pointless, and Nora was cold and exhausted. "Can you find prints on the cuff link?"

Rush inhaled and rubbed his chin, then exhaled. His shoulders relaxed. "Doubtful. But I'll try. I'll try everything." He held her gaze and she fidgeted. Angry at him or not, she wasn't blind. The man was attractive. Always had been.

"How did you find the car?" It had been seventeen years. Why now?

"You remember Brandon Deerborn?"

Few years ahead of them. "Yeah."

"His son was doing a project using Google maps and our town. Found the lake and noticed something in it. Like a shimmer, he said. He went out there, climbed a pine to check it out—fell out of the tree by the way and broke his arm…also he's grounded for leaving without asking—and Brandon called me. Put the divers in and we hauled it out. Water was too murky to notice it at ground level."

"Google maps. Invasive yet…" She shrugged. "He might be grounded but he'll be a town hero." Or maybe not. If what people said about Mom was true, there'd be a few who wouldn't be too thrilled the Deerborn kid had found her.

Rush didn't say anything and kept his eyes on the sky.

"Storm's coming in. But I guess you know this already." He smirked.

She grinned, then sobered. "I'm serious about investigating. I want answers before I leave here, and I won't bring up our past again. Better if we leave things on the personal side alone. Focus on the case."

"We don't have a case. Yet." The freezing rain slacked up.

"Never hurts to ask questions."

"Yes, it does. Sometimes." Rush shoved his gloved hands in his pockets. "Go home. Be with your family. I'll call you tomorrow."

He was right. Nothing she could do tonight. She walked back to her car, opened the door when Rush called out. "Nora Beth, be careful. The roads are slick. Watch for deer."

Her middle name was Jane, but Rush had never once used it. A little nod to *Little House on the Prairie*. In high school, she'd forced him to watch reruns, but there hadn't been much Rush wouldn't have done for her. Manly called Laura *Beth*. Only him. Rush had started that at fifteen. It warmed the chill seeping into Nora's bones. "Will do."

She climbed inside and blasted the heat. She'd regretted pushing Rush away after Mom vanished. She'd been hurt. Wanted a fresh start, to pretend she lived in a town where gossip about Mom hadn't abounded. Where she didn't feel shame. But coming home after college—she'd missed Rush so much it ached—she thought he might be willing to give it another chance, and if so she'd stay. And he'd done the one thing she'd worked hard to avoid—made her the subject of ugly rumors.

She drove carefully through the winding roads and spotted Mom's favorite café. Charlee, the owner, might know a thing or two. Inside, Charlee met her with a wave. "Well, look who the cat dragged in." Her face paled. "Sorry. Bad use of words. I heard about your mama. I'm so sorry." She poured a steaming cup of coffee and slid it to Nora as she sat on the bar stool.

"Thanks. Did you know anything about that night? Why my mom might be heading out of town or be near the lake?"

"I wish I did, hon. I loved Marilyn, but she only let one get so close before she distanced herself."

Nora sipped the brew and talked with Charlee until the weather picked up. "I better get on back. If anything comes to mind, call me."

Charlee nodded. "Be safe, Nora."

Nora inched along the roads until, almost thirty minutes later, her father's vast lodge peeped out from the evergreens. A wintry, dark sky overhead seemed to close in on the structure that housed two hundred and fifty-two guests. Nestled in the mountains behind were fifty chalets. Every room, every wooden cottage would be occupied, except the guest chalet where she liked to stay.

White lights clinked in the trees as gusts of wind barreled through the pines. The smell of evergreen, wood smoke and cinnamon wafted into her car—the smell of home. She stepped out of the car, pinched the bridge of her nose, inhaled deeply and trudged up the walk; someone had plowed the drive for her. Fresh snow hadn't quite blanketed it again. Something stole her nose's attention. She sniffed. Was that paint? She followed the scent to the side of the chalet and gasped.

In the moonlight, she made out one of her two most hated words to call women along with a note painted underneath telling her to die like her mother. Shock sucked the breath from her, and then she caught sight of a shadow moving toward her. She had only seconds to block the blow and failed.

A meaty fist covered in camouflage gloves connected with her face, knocking her into two feet of snow. White spots popped in front of her eyes and her head spun.

"Take the warning and take a hike," the masked man growled. "Or you'll regret it."

His feet crunched along the snow.

Buzzing whizzed in her ears and then silence.

When her eyes fluttered open, a man had her. Panic shot through her system and she flailed, scratched and punched.

"Hey, hey! Nora. It's me. It's Rush. You're safe. You're safe."

Rush. Rush punched her? No. Her head was fuzzy and aching. Rush had her in his arms. It felt familiar, but also strangely new and wonderfully safe and warm. Her stomach dipped and as if he could feel her thoughts, he nestled her closer against him.

"I got hit," she croaked.

His grip tightened. "And I'll be sure to return the favor when I find the guy." His tone was raw steel. She laid her head against his chest, heard the staccato beat of his heart. "Did you see him?"

"No. Just the writing on the wall, and then he stuck it to me and knocked me out." Her limbs were numb and stiff. Her teeth chattered. Rush carried her up the porch steps.

"Do you need a doctor?"

"No. It's no worse than when I got bucked off that horse that time."

"You had a mild concussion then, Nora Beth." Rush chuckled and swung open the front door and stepped inside, then flipped on a lamp on the side table.

"Right. Not the best comparison. Well, I'm fine. Honest. Just sore." She peered into his rich eyes and nearly got lost. Certainly got choked up.

He laid her on the soft leather sofa and tucked a strand of hair behind her ear. "I'll get your bags. You need to get into dry, warm clothes and I'll start a fire for extra heat." He stepped outside before she could speak, brought in her luggage and carried it to her bedroom, then returned. "Make some coffee. Yeah?"

She nodded.

"Sure you don't need a doctor?" He touched her face. "Lying in the snow probably helped the swelling, but…"

She shivered and he pointed to the bedroom. "We'll talk in a minute. Or I can take you to the hospital."

Shaking her head, she shuffled to the bed and he closed the door. If Rush hadn't come to her rescue… She didn't want to think about what might have happened.

Clearly, she'd angered someone. But who? She'd seen dozens of locals on the scene; they'd heard her rant. By now, Nora sticking around to find out what happened that night was bound to be spreading all over Splendor Pines like lice in a day care. Between talking to Rush, leaving the scene, stopping to talk to Charlee—someone had rallied fast. Not fast enough or Nora wouldn't have walked up on them.

After throwing on sweats, wool socks and an oversize Vols sweatshirt, she looked in the mirror. No swelling but her right cheek had a purplish tint. Wood smoke and coffee brewing drew her into the living room decorated in cozy earth tones. The fire reached out and hugged her cold skin. She inched closer to the large brick hearth and sat.

"How you feelin'?" Rush made himself at home in the open kitchen. He took two white mugs from the cabinet and poured the coffee, then opened the fridge and frowned. He rifled in the other cabinets until he found powdered creamer and sugar. He carried everything to the living room and placed them on the coffee table.

"Oh, ya know…like I got punched and knocked into the snow." She touched her cheek.

"What exactly happened?"

She gave him the rundown. "Told me to back off or I'd end up like my mom. Almost did if you hadn't shown up. Why are you here?"

His neck flushed as he handed her a cup of coffee. "Honestly? I don't know. I guess to check in on you."

Whatever the reason, she was thankful. She added cream and sugar to her cup.

"You recognize the voice by any chance?" Rush hurriedly asked, as if hoping to skim over the topic of his popping in.

"No. I was kind of busy being terrified. Sorry."

Rush sat beside her, laid a gentle hand on her knee. "I'm sorry too."

Half of her wanted to jerk his hand away, but the frightened half needed the tender contact, the reassurance and compassion. He removed his hand and she sipped her coffee, relishing the warmth of the fire and the brew.

The fire crackled.

He studied the purple mark on her face and balled a fist. "Nora, I don't think it's a good idea for you to go poking around after what happened. This is my job. Better to let me handle it."

Nora huffed. "Someone doesn't want me looking into my mother's death. Which means it might not have been an accident. More than ever, I have to."

Rush drank his coffee and kept quiet, his jaw slowly working.

"What's the matter? I know that face."

Rush pinched the bridge of his nose. "Everything is the matter, Nora Beth. From the minute we pulled the car from the water to right this second. No, it might not have been an accident, but chances are it was, and this attack on you might be from someone who is afraid you'll discover…you know…an affair. If even a quarter of the rumors are true, then there are a lot of people who won't want the past hauled into the present. Next time it might not be a punch to the face." He skimmed the bruise with his fingertips, bringing a wave of emotion she'd tried to bury years ago.

She turned away enough to force him to keep his hands to himself. She didn't need the attraction or the old feelings. But he did have a point. "Then those men shouldn't have had those affairs. What happened to nobility, fidelity and honesty? If their dirty secrets get exposed, then so be it. They shouldn't have done it." Mom shouldn't have either. Why would she?

Rush's nostrils flared, but he didn't respond.

"What happens when *you* investigate? Secrets will be exposed. One way or the other."

He drained his coffee and set the cup on the hearth. "I'm not worried about my safety. I am worried about yours. Besides, I'm going to be more discreet than you."

"You're going to have to talk to more than men you suspect could be guilty. You'll have to talk to neighbors, friends and, sadly, wives. It is what it is. I don't want to hurt people. But I do want the truth about that night. Someone has answers to my thousands of questions."

One being why Dad never stayed on top of the investigation. Why didn't he hire a private eye? Was he glad to be rid of Mom? Was he tired of having an unfaithful wife? Nora couldn't ignore these rumors like she had as a teenager. They were staring her down and now that she'd been attacked and told to back off, denying that even one of them were true would be naive. *Mom, why? Did you not love Dad?* He was amazing and wonderful. He gave them everything.

Or maybe Nora was only seeing what she wanted to see.

A faithful mom.

A devoted husband.

Maybe neither were who they seemed.

"What if you never find out why your mom was heading out of town?"

"How do you know she was?"

Rush stood and turned away from her. "Because we found two cases in the trunk. One had clothing in it." He faced her. "She was going somewhere, Nora."

Nora's hands trembled, and she steadied her cup between her knees.

"I know that's not what you want to hear. And you have to understand that no matter what turns up, you won't get every single answer to your questions. And that's not even the most frightening part of this."

"No?" She peered into his eyes, firelight casting shadows on his face. "What is?"

"You won't back down, and I don't believe whoever did this to you is going to back down either. Which means you're not safe as long as you're snooping."

Nora swallowed the fear clawing in her throat. "I can't sit back and do nothing."

He collapsed beside her again and groaned. "I had a feeling you'd say that. I think you should stay up at the main house. You'll be safer there."

Her first instinct was to say no, but Rush was right. However… "Hailey is staying with my dad. Which means

Dalton is also. He's only six. If someone comes after me again, he could be in harm's way. Hailey too. While I agree that I should stay at the main house, it scares me not to stay here." Scared her to stay here too.

"I heard she was living back home for a while."

Nora shrugged. "I don't suppose any marriage is perfect. Except maybe your mom and dad's."

Rush grunted. What did that mean? Bringing up Rush's parents gave her an idea. "Hey, your dad was a part-time deputy back then. I remember him coming to talk to my dad. Maybe he knows something about that night or he overheard a conversation that would help. We should talk to him."

Rush's jaw flinched. "Yeah… I'll talk to him."

Nora wasn't so sure she believed him. Something was up with his parents, but now wasn't the time to pry. She had to stay somewhere safe. The main house wasn't it. "I can't stay at the main house. Just in case. Besides, Dad has security that patrols all night. Guests love added security measures."

Wind howled and sleet started up again, pelting the windows. "I don't like it, but I understand. Take my number. Call me if you need anything. Anytime of night."

Rush rattled off his number.

Nora laughed. "Seriously? The last four digits of your number is four, five, six, seven?"

"Hard to memorize, huh?" he teased.

"It's probably the only number in my phone I can." She saved his contact information and closed her eyes. "Rush, you do think it's only a threat, right? No one will actually try to kill me?"

Rush stopped at the front door, raised his coat's wool collar. "Nora, you're about to unleash an avalanche. What do you think?" He bent over and lifted his pant leg, retrieving a handgun from an ankle holster. "This is my personal piece. Lock the doors and keep it on your nightstand."

Nora accepted the gun and prayed she wouldn't have to use it. "Rush?"

He turned before leaving. "Yeah?"

"You said two cases. What was in the other one?"

"It was your mom's camera case." His mouth formed a grim line. "With two hundred and fifty thousand dollars inside."

TWO

"How'd you sleep, honey?" Dad looked up from his desk with tired eyes.

"I'm guessing about like you. Harrison stopped in at first light." Dad's Chief of Security had scared her half to death. He ought to be thankful he's alive. She almost shot him.

"I should have called and told you he'd be by to paint over the graffiti. I wanted it done before too many people saw it. I'm sorry that happened." He scooted out from his mahogany leather chair and crossed the room. Dressy jeans. Dress shirt that brought out the lighter flecks of brown in his eyes. She'd always wished she'd been blessed with her father's eyes. He opened his arms to her, as he always did.

She walked into them and let his comfort shield her and make her feel safe. A different safety than how she felt in Rush's arms last night. She didn't want to think too much on that. There was nothing left between her and Rush romantically.

"I had him put more security around the chalet for you." He touched the tender area on her cheek. "Rush taking care of this?"

"He is." She pulled away, cleared her throat. "Dad,

I've never asked because I never wanted to know. Or I didn't believe. But after last night there has to be some truth to the gossip." She peered into his eyes, waiting for the bomb to drop.

Dad didn't speak for what seemed like an eternity. He touched her shoulder; his eyes held a mix of resolve and sadness. "Nora, why don't you remember your mother in all the good ways like Friday manicures and pancakes on Sunday. Or even that silly song she sang to help you sleep that only made you giggle and stay up longer. I think she did that deliberately to have more time with you. Don't try to pull up anything ugly. You'll find no peace there."

Nora held back the burning tears. Those were the memories fueling her search for truth. Mom had loved her, but did she ever love Dad? "You're not denying it. Is that why you didn't go on a mad hunt to find her after she disappeared? Were you relieved she was gone?"

Dad's jaw ticked and he inhaled sharply. "I loved your mother, Nora. The only relief I have is that now I have some closure. Let Rush look into who assaulted you and vandalized my property, but as far as the past, you stay out of it."

Nora had zero closure. *Stay out of it?*

Dad wasn't going to give her any answers; no point in bringing up the fact Mom had a huge sum of money in the camera case. If he did know about it, he wouldn't tell her. Nora had searching to do. Searching no one else seemed to want to do. Rush believed the past was an accident. He wouldn't put the proper time into it. Someone needed to fight for the truth.

"Now, why are you really here?" he asked. "I'm thrilled to have you. I hate that you came home to this."

"Can't a girl come home longer than Christmas Day?"

She didn't have the courage to admit the truth. Besides, he was keeping secrets of his own.

He raised a dark eyebrow but didn't push. "You can always come home, honey."

"I know." Outside the sky was painted gray. Trendy on walls. Gloomy in her heart. "We'll have snow again soon. More rain and ice too."

"Knock, knock." Rush rapped on the side of the door frame. In uniform. He'd shaved and his fresh, soft cheeks held the dimples she'd always loved. "I see you got the spray paint covered up. You wanna report it officially?"

Joshua nodded. "Absolutely. I'll go down to the station this afternoon. I put Harrison and the night security on more rounds, especially at the chalet."

"Good." Rush cleared his throat and glanced at Nora. "How's the noggin?"

"Thinking about the next step." In between the thumping. "Which is breakfast," she added.

He chuckled. "I'll walk you down to the dining area, if that's okay."

"See you tonight," she said to her dad.

"Honey, remember our conversation."

She would. But it wasn't going to change her mind. As they walked down the hall to the elevator, she spoke. "Dad thinks I should back off. But why wouldn't he want to know what happened that night?"

Rush hit the elevator button. "He might want to spare himself further pain. Or he could know more than he's letting on to spare *your* feelings. Sometimes people keep secrets to protect loved ones." They stepped in and he pushed the first floor to go up from the basement offices.

"Secrets don't protect people. They hurt people." She slid him a sideways glance. He'd kept the fact he was dating Ainsley from her, and it hadn't spared her feelings.

It had hurt more than anything. Her secrets of why she was back now would hurt and disappoint Dad.

They stepped off the elevator and took in the beautiful snowcapped view from the wall of windows that lined the hall and the dining area.

"I'm going to try to follow that money trail, Rush. It came from somewhere. If I can track it, I can get answers."

Rush pulled a chair out for her and sat across from her. She didn't miss his grimace. "I reviewed the initial police report from when she went missing, and the follow-up notes from Sheriff Parsons. Nothing about money. Nothing at all that would be a lead."

"What did your dad say?"

Rush unrolled his silverware, a grim expression. "I haven't had time to talk to him."

"You haven't had time?" She stared at him dumbfounded.

Rush balled his fist on the table. "Anything he would know would have been put in the report, Nora. And I was a little busy last night taking care of you."

Nora counted to ten. Rush had rescued and protected her. "Okay. But I still want you to talk to him. Or I can—"

"I'll do it. I'll do it."

The server came and Rush ordered coffee and toast. Nora ordered pecan pancakes with vanilla syrup and a side of bacon. She ate when she was wound up. She shivered and scanned the room. No one looked suspicious, but she couldn't shake the feeling of being watched.

When the server left the table, Rush continued. "Right now, I need you to be objective. Think back. Do you remember your parents ever fighting? Especially within a day or two of the ball?"

Nora shook her head and sipped her Irish breakfast

tea with honey. "My parents never fought. I mean, if they did, then they kept it from me and Hailey. Plenty of space around here to raise voices and no one but the mountains to hear." She leaned forward. "Why? Do you think my dad had anything to do with this? I mean, I know he hasn't searched hard, but to murder my mom?"

"Whoa!" Rush put his hands up. "Don't jump to conclusions and certainly not out loud where diners can hear. I never said that." He scowled across the table.

"Well, you certainly implied it."

He shifted in his seat. "I didn't mean to. I'm saying if you could remember them arguing, you might remember some of the dialogue, which might be helpful."

She couldn't drum up one heated conversation. "Maybe he didn't know she was having affairs."

Rush gave her the get-real face. "Rumors flew through town. There's no way he hadn't heard them. Possibly approached her. A man was in that car at some point that night or around the event. Could be he caught her with him that night."

And did what? "For not meaning to imply, you're doing it again."

Rush's neck reddened. "We need to find the man who owns the cuff link and mask. He might have answers. We can get photos from the party."

"Silver cuff links aren't rare. And what if the wearer isn't in the pictures?"

Rush tented his hands on the table. "I'd like them anyway."

Nora nodded as the food arrived. They waited for the server to leave before going back into their discussion. "They'd be in a storage room near the offices. I can get them for you later today."

They made small talk, dancing around the past.

"How's Hailey?" Rush asked.

"I think she's keeping a brave front for Dalton since he's already going through a lot." She added more syrup to her pancakes. "How's your family?"

Rush's jaw ticked. "Fine. Everyone's coming in for the Christmas celebration."

"Greer and Hollister?"

Rush's eyes held surprise. "You remember them?"

"How could I forget?" She remembered all those summers with Rush, including the ones with his cousins.

His phone rang and he answered; a few minutes later he hung up. "I have to go. With this weather, all hands are on deck with traffic accidents and we have one on Route 5. Turned into a brawl. Let me pay for my breakfast."

"Toast is twenty-two fifty." She held in a giggle.

Rush paused, then grinned. She'd had a weak spot for that killer smile. Guess she hadn't done enough strength training lately. It was making its mark.

"Don't worry about it. Daddy would be fit to be tied if he knew you were paying for meals here." She bit into her bacon. "I'll bring the photos by the station in a couple of hours."

"Be careful. Clearly the roads are treacherous, not to mention other dangers."

"Will do." She saluted him with the bacon but lost her appetite. Someone wasn't going to be pleased when they found out she wasn't giving up the quest for truth. She rubbed her cheek and shivered, then made her way down to the offices and storage rooms where they kept the predigitalized masquerade photos for marketing purposes. She flipped the light switch. The fluorescent lights flickered and hummed, only two lighting the dim room.

Using her cell phone flashlight, she crept into the room, highlighting the dates on cardboard boxes. Like something out of a TV show evidence facility. Dust sent her into a wave of sneezes. Halfway down the fourth aisle, she found the box. "Bingo."

A noise came from behind. Mouse? *Please be a mouse.*

Hairs rose on her arms and neck. She turned as a masked man snatched the box of photos and shoved her to the ground.

No! Nora jumped up, adrenaline pumping. With all her might, she pushed until the metal row in front of her toppled and crashed onto the masked man, boxes spilling open as papers and photos littered the concrete floor.

Nora hurdled over the boxes and debris, hands shaking, and grabbed the box he'd dropped, then ran like the wind. With one hand, she dialed 911. The dispatcher answered. Menacing words and papers shuffled in the distance. *Oh, no.* "Tell Rush Buchanan to get to Pine Refuge Resort and Lodge." The attacker was on her tail. "Basement. Storage room. Now! Right now! This is Nora…" The phone slipped from her shaking hands as she took a hard right. Could she make the elevator? No. Where? Where could she go?

Custodial closet. Down the next hall.

She gripped the box. The attacker gained on her. She ran hard enough her chin shook.

Five feet.

Four.

Two…

She flew into the room, closed the door and locked it. The attacker banged and pulled on the knob. Could he find a way in? Could she find a way out? A small rectangular window above was covered in snow. The box wouldn't fit through it. She could escape and leave the photos, but if he got inside he'd have them, and obviously something in them incriminated someone or he wouldn't want the box so badly.

Her phone was gone.

No way to communicate. She curled into a ball until the banging and twisting on the doorknob silenced. Was he gone? Was he waiting on her to open the door?

What could be in these photos? And how did the attacker know she'd be in the storage room?

Chills slithered across her spine.

She had been watched.

"Nora! Nora Beth!" Rush stormed down the hall. Millie at Dispatch had called him, and what should have been a ten-minute drive had taken him over twenty thanks to the road conditions that were worsening each hour. Rush's heart pounded in his chest as he hunted for Nora. *God, please keep her protected.* He'd made his way to the storage room and taken in the disaster.

"Nora!"

He headed right, down another hall.

"Nora!"

"Rush. Rush!" The custodial closet door opened and Nora flew into his arms, gripping with all her might. "A man tried to steal the photos." Her shoulders relaxed and she explained what happened.

Rush brushed a strand of blond hair from her face and tucked it safely behind her ear. His gaze locked on hers and he couldn't quite make out what swam in her watery blue-greens—relief but something else.

"I was so scared I didn't know what to do."

"You did the right thing calling, then locking yourself in here." More than ever they needed those photos. Rush needed to find all the Phantom of the Opera masked men. One of them had answers or could be the one trying to hurt Nora. "Let's find your phone, get these and you somewhere safe." He grabbed the box.

Troy wouldn't want him exhausting his energy on this. As far as he was concerned, it was a closed case. He'd agreed with Rush that someone wasn't happy about Nora turning over rocks and they should be looking into that. But after two attacks and being followed, Rush wasn't so sure it was all about a possible scandal. People had killed for less, though.

The only place he knew the photos would be safe was under his care, at his house. He wasn't sure he wanted Nora there permeating it with her sweet cherry blossom scent and intensifying his loneliness when she left.

Rush led Nora to his vehicle and opened the door for her, then put the photos in the backseat. He hurried inside, cranked the heat and sighed. "You okay with going to my place?"

"Sure." Her cheeks turned pink and she gazed out the window. "I heard you built a house on the mountain."

"About four years ago. Still needs some work, but I'm only one man."

"Who's saved me twice. Thank you." She rubbed her palms together.

Rush pointed all the vents toward her. "You'd think tourists would stop pouring in. This keeps up and flights won't only be delayed, they'll be canceled."

"People pay good money to be here on the holidays. They don't care about the weather. Sometimes I feel like I'm talking to nothing *but* the camera."

Rush switched his wipers on to knock away the ice pelting the windshield. The rest of the ride was fairly quiet. He turned onto a long drive that cut up through a thick forest of evergreens. His two-story A-frame log cabin with a deck wrapped around the entire second story came into view. He loved having coffee out there and seeing the mountains for miles. It was peaceful and quiet.

And empty.

"Wow, Rush. I love how it's covered in windows. So much natural light, and what a view from up here." Nora gaped and took it all in. He felt that way every day.

He parked out front, grabbed the box and they went inside. Nora studied the cedar beams and walls. The kitchen was open to the living room. Leather furniture. Rugs for warmth on the knotty pine flooring.

"I love what you've done with it." She frowned. "Where's your Christmas tree?"

"I didn't put one up this year." One tree decorated for one man? Seemed silly.

She gasped. "Rush!"

"Did you put a tree up at your place in Knoxville?"

She collapsed on the couch. "No, but I haven't put a tree up since Mom disappeared…died." Tears leaked from her eyes, and she wiped them away with her sweater sleeves that hung over her fingertips. "You have no reason not to."

"Neither do you," he said delicately. "She wouldn't have wanted you to stop loving and celebrating your favorite holiday. Besides you're celebrating Christ's birth."

"Which doesn't call for a tree."

"You put up a nativity?"

"No. Make me some coffee and let's go through photos." She grinned and headed for the box on the kitchen counter.

"You're bossy."

"You ought to know." She slid the lid off the box. "Hey, Rush?"

"Hmm…?" He opened a bin and took a K-Cup for the Keurig.

"Nothing." Fear pulsed in her eyes. Whatever she was about to open up and say, she'd bit back.

"You can talk to me, you know. Like you used to." Before her world crumbled and she closed herself off.

"It's nothing."

Frustration knotted his neck and shoulder muscles. He gave her a cup of coffee how she liked it, with cream and sugar, and started combing through photos. He searched for men in Phantom of the Opera masks. "Do you know where there might be other photos? Not every single person is going to turn up in this box." Hundreds of people attended each Christmas. Several hundred of them local, and nearly three hundred tourists. This was a needle in a haystack job.

"Tourist center might have some put away. Locals probably have personal scrapbooks. What are we even looking for?" Nora asked, and thumbed through the photos.

"The mask in the car was a partial of the Phantom of the Opera. Look for men wearing that." He left out the other reason it was important. How did one tell an ex-girlfriend he'd seen her mom kissing the Phantom? She'd been through so much already. "And someone with silver cuff links."

"My dad wore cuff links but not like those." She held up a photo. "Look, it's you and Dan in those ridiculous masks with whisker-like things growing out of the sides." She laughed, but he heard the bittersweet tone.

"Good times." Rush couldn't manage much more. That was the night his dream shattered. He found two photos of two different men in Phantom masks. One seemed like it might be Ward McKay. He owned McKay Construction and was divorced. Could Marilyn be the rift that caused it? "Did you ever hear talk about Ward McKay and your mom?"

Nora paused perusing. "I steered clear of talk if I could."

"His wife moved away with their son. He might have been pretty mad over that even though it would have been his fault. Anger brings irrational behavior and thoughts sometimes." He couldn't believe he said that. He had no facts to support that theory. "I'm speculating and really I shouldn't be."

"No," Nora said. "That makes sense."

If Ward was the Phantom kissing Marilyn three months after he had separated from his wife, he might have wanted a more permanent relationship with Marilyn. If she rejected that, after he lost his family for her, that could have sent him over the edge. She might have been escaping him. Or something more sinister.

But they didn't have proof that Marilyn's car in the lake was intentional. And he was only speculating again. "If the car wreck was an accident, then all we're doing is meddling in people's lives to give you some comfort." A lot of damage could be done. "Is that fair?"

Nora jutted her chin toward him and glared. "What if it was your mother?"

He didn't know. Before his dad falsely accused a man of soliciting a prostitute, which ended up causing the man to commit suicide, he'd have said yes. But now? Now he wasn't so sure he'd go around prying.

"We have to question Ward, Rush. Evidence or not. What's he got to lose now?" Nora asked.

"If your mom's death wasn't an accident, then a lot."

THREE

The winter storm had slacked off, leaving a foot of fresh powdered snow and temperatures in the low twenties. But it wasn't keeping tourists and locals away from Main Street. Carolers dressed in Victorian clothing wassailed along singing inside the shops that were lit with candles and twinkling lights. Nora loved the candle store best with its cranberry, pine and cinnamon scents that wafted through the air. She'd be buying one of the candles when they got there. Small stations were set up for tourists to relax and revel with mulled cider or cocoa. With red noses and wrapped head to toe like mummies in winter garb and bags loading them down, people were having a ball.

Road crews had done a good job of clearing the roads and sidewalks. Nora and Hailey walked with Dalton, his lips coated in chocolate and whipped cream. Nora had missed so much of his growing up by only visiting once a year. She'd forgotten how much she loved these pre-Christmas festivities. They'd bumped into several people Nora had grown up with, and there had been no narrowed eyes or questions about Mom, but Nora couldn't help but feel gawked at. Rush had been called away due to shoplifters, and being here in public, Nora didn't think anyone would try something. She hoped anyway. She had her sister and Dalton with her.

"Nora, do you think you should push this?" Making a motion with her chin toward Dalton, Hailey let Nora know to talk in code so young ears didn't hear.

"Don't you want answers?"

"Yes, but not enough to bring on the extra trouble, if you know what I mean. Maybe we should move on. I don't care to know about every single indiscretion, and quite frankly, I believe there were many."

"But why? What was so bad in the marriage that would cause that?"

Hailey sighed and watched as Dalton jetted ahead, gawking in the taffy store. "People grow apart, Nora. They live in the same house, share the bills and running errands and after-school activities, but the spark dies."

"I'm sorry about you and Nate."

Hailey squeezed her hand but said nothing.

Nora had seen marriages that lasted. Burned bright all through the years. Rush's parents for one. And her grandparents on Dad's side. Mom had no family. No pictures. They'd burned in a house fire when Mom was young.

Hair rose on her neck and she scanned the area.

"So how are things with you and Rush?" Hailey asked.

Nora shook off the feeling of being watched again. "Fine. Good." He was helping her look into a case. That's it. Although sitting in his home, drinking coffee and reminiscing over old photos had shifted the place where she kept her feelings for him confined. "To be honest, I wish he'd be more aggressive on this investigation. He acts like he can't question anyone until he has proof, but he can't get proof without asking questions. It's like people who need their first job but can't get one without experience. How do you gain experience if you can't get a job?"

Hailey snorted. "You're babbling."

"I suppose I am." Rush frustrated her with his tippy-toeing around. She was beginning to think he was pacifying her with his promises to look into the past. He hadn't done much of anything.

They stopped inside the candle shop and Nora bought an orange-cranberry candle. Outside, Nora spotted Candace Fick. "Hey, didn't she and Mom have lunches every Thursday afternoon?"

"Yeah, but that doesn't mean she knows any more than we do."

Carolers crooned, "Have Yourself a Merry Little Christmas."

"You never know. I'm gonna hop over and see if we can have a lunch of our own. I'll be right back."

Blue lights flashed in the distance. Looked like Rush's Bronco inching its way up the road. Butterflies swam in her stomach. Oh, no. No. No. She was not going to let herself swoon over him. For many reasons. One, she wasn't even staying in Splendor Pines. She was moving to Florida—hopefully.

Two, he'd cheated on Ainsley, and if he'd cheat on her what was to say he wouldn't cheat on Nora someday? There was no guarantee. And worst-case scenario, what if the rumors about her mother were true? What if Nora had her genes? Because if she were being honest she'd have to admit that even if she had known Rush was dating Ainsley, it wouldn't have stopped her from spending time with him, holding his hand, embracing him, cuddling on the couch or even kissing him.

She was pulled from the souring thought. Literally.

A meaty hand yanked her by the collar behind the shops, thrusting her up against the brick, her face scraping against the rough exterior. "I told you to back off!"

he hissed, and cut off her scream with his thick gloved hand. She flailed and elbowed him in the chest, but his heavy coat must have taken most of the blow. It barely slowed him down. Adrenaline coursed through her veins; blood swooshed in her temples.

He yanked a strand of lights from the trim of the building and wound them around her throat, tightening them. She couldn't breathe! She grabbed at them, the twinkling rainbow hot around her neck and flashing in her eyes. In the distance, carolers sang, "O Christmas Tree." A serenade to her—Nora the human Christmas tree.

Help! Someone!

The cord dug into her neck, stinging. Her eyes watered and her throat swelled. Blood heated in her cheeks.

Using her foot, she back kicked him. She missed his groin and knocked his upper thigh. He cursed and thrust her to the ground, never releasing his grip on her throat with the lights.

Spots formed in front of her eyes.

The snow burned cold on her cheek.

He practically sat on her back as if he was roping a calf. She felt along the snow and found her bag with the candle.

"Nora?"

Rush!

The attacker released his grip enough for her to gulp a breath of air and wiggle around to use the candle as a weapon. She held the handles of the plastic bag and swung it like a bat against the side of his face; he groaned and jumped off her.

Rush moved in on him, but he scrambled and found his footing, racing ahead into the crowd. Rush radioed their location as he gave chase. She coughed and unwound the Christmas lights from her neck, breathing in the cold, fresh winter air.

Jogging, Rush came back to her and knelt. "Are you okay?"

No. But she had to show a sign of strength. "Just need to catch my breath."

He tipped her chin, searched her eyes. "Nora, be honest." Concern pulsed in his. "Talk to me."

"I'm fine." She hid her shaking hands. "How'd you find me?"

Rush blew a heavy sigh. "Hailey said you went to talk to Candace Fick, but Candace said she never saw you. I got a gut feeling. Went looking for you from point A to B."

Nora rubbed the tender area on her neck. "Anyone tell you that you ought to be in law enforcement? Private Eye? Detective? Human Metal Detector?"

"I'm glad you can find the funny in this."

Nothing about this was funny, but she didn't want to admit she might have bitten off more than she could chew. Because she couldn't back down regardless.

"That's me. The funny girl."

Rush pulled Nora to her feet. He brushed a gloved thumb across her cheek. "Nora, this is getting out of hand and I'm worried."

Join the club. "I'll be okay. I've got you around." She tried to play it off lightheartedly but it fell flat.

"I'm not always around, though. If I hadn't been just down the street…"

She'd be dead right now. With no answers. She didn't want to think about it. "Candace might know where Mom was going that night or who had been with her. They were friends."

"Why hasn't she come forward, then?" Rush asked.

"I don't know." Nora picked up the bag with the candle inside, brushed snow from it.

Rush pointed to the sleigh rides. "Why don't we take a break and hitch a ride back to the lodge."

"Isn't your Bronco still here?"

"Don't want to go 'dashing through the snow in a one-horse open sleigh' with me?" Rush winked and slung his arm around Nora's shoulders.

"As long as we don't have to laugh all the way. My ribs won't take it." She ignored her heart's warning to abandon his protective arms and charm and she leaned into him. Rumors were sure to abound.

Snuggled under a quilt with Nora on the sleigh ride had brought back so many memories. Rush had been smitten with her since he made fun of her pink sparkly tennis shoes in third grade and she shoved him down the hill on the playground. She'd been full of spunk and spice and still was. Normally, he'd appreciate that but it was fueling her need to keep pushing into the past. She didn't trust him to do his job, and coupled with refusing to let her feelings out, it was utterly disappointing. Didn't she see they were in this together?

Nora's father stood on the steps of the chalet as the sleigh ride came to its end. Rush had texted him ten minutes earlier and filled him in on the newest attack.

He met Nora as she stepped out and drew her into his arms. "Nora, how many times am I going to have to beg you to stop this? It's going to get you killed."

She didn't respond but pulled from his embrace.

Joshua's nostrils flared, but underneath the anger was fear. Fear for his daughter. "I've given the family staying next to you an upgraded chalet. Rush, you take that one until you don't need it anymore. I understand appearances." He peered into Nora's eyes. "But if you won't come back to the main house and let me take care of you, then I'll feel better knowing Rush is six feet away. But again, I wish you'd come up to the house and let Rush look into the attacks. If you stop digging, they might stop."

Rush thought the same thing, but the killer may believe Nora found the incriminating photo. If so, he would be coming to silence her for it. Rush too.

Nora looked at her dad and then at Rush. "If the results come back that there is no foul play involved, I'll consider it. But something bad happened that night. I know it."

Rush believed it too. He didn't think Nora would consider letting it go. He shook Joshua's hand. "I appreciate the chalet. I'll get my things later."

They stood quietly, a bit awkward, then Joshua tightened his scarf. "I've got some work to do." He left them on Nora's porch.

"What now?" Nora asked.

"We compile a list of names we heard rumors about and quietly investigate to see if they were true. Then we add their wives to that list. You know the phrase about women scorned."

"They buy Ben & Jerry's?" A slender eyebrow twitched north, giving Nora a sly, flirty look.

Heat swarmed Rush's gut. "Something like that."

Nora unlocked the chalet and they stepped into the warmth. She hung her coat on the hook by the front door and dropped her purse, hat and gloves on the kitchen counter, then lit the candle she'd wielded as a weapon earlier. Didn't take long for the chalet to become enveloped in orange and cranberry with a hint of cinnamon.

"We should make a list of the people who were there when the car was taken from the lake too," she said. "I always stay at the guest chalet. Someone knew it, knew I was home and that I was coming after them. Had to be someone who was there."

"Not necessarily. Anyone could have picked up the phone to gossip and shared it with the wrong—or right—person. I'll work on the men with rumored affairs and their wives." He'd spare her that dreaded deed. "After I build a fire."

"I'll make coffee."

They went to work on their tasks, then sat on opposite ends of the sofa, notebooks in hand, stopping every once in a while to pour more coffee. Nora pulled a box of ginger snaps from the cupboard that had been stocked. Rush was thankful for them; he hadn't eaten dinner.

"I only have about ten people on my list, and I know more were at the lake that night." Nora tapped her lead pencil on the notebook and scowled. He'd always loved her perturbed look. It made her nose perkier and her full lips poutier.

He tried to ignore his attraction and focus on the work. "Read off the names and let's see if any of them match mine, then we'll circle them and put them at the top of our suspect list."

Nora smirked. "You got it, Matlock."

Rush chuckled and Nora read her list. He circled the names she called out that he had on his list of rumored affairs: Ward McKay, Len Franklin and Harvey Langston. He still had three more names on his list. Martin Hassleback, Kent Sammons and Rodney Jones.

"Let's start with the first three we matched and then move on with the other three. Ward, Harvey, Len and Martin are divorced so they rank even higher as the chances of the rumors being true are greater," Rush said.

Nora rolled her pencil along her bottom lip. He cleared

his throat. "I'm only speculating. Don't take it as the gospel truth."

"Why do you keep prefacing your speculations or putting that addendum on there? Cops speculate, Rush. It's not like you're accusing anyone of anything…yet." Nora laid her notepad and pencil on the coffee table, stretched and yawned.

"I don't want to falsely accuse anyone of something. It could wreck them." And himself.

"Fine, but we have to process our ideas. I'm not going to go out there and tell the world these things."

No, just the men whose names are on the list. And if they didn't have an affair, it might circulate once again and marriages could fall apart and worse. Rush's cell phone rang. Gary Plenk. "It's the coroner."

"Put him on speaker," Nora said.

"Hey, Gary, what's up? You're on speaker with myself and Nora Livingstone."

There was a pause on the line. Gary had bad news. Rush glanced at Nora and she nodded. "It's okay, Gary, you can say what you need to say."

"I'm so sorry, Nora. The DNA was conclusive."

"I was prepared for that. Thank you," Nora said but her voice choked up and she stared at the floor.

"Uh… Rush, could we talk a minute?" Gary asked.

Nora held up her hand and shook her head. Words wouldn't come. Right now, he wanted to tell Gary to call back later, take Nora into his arms and comfort her, but he doubted she'd let him. She may have been prepared for this call, but the reality was Marilyn was gone. Forever. It was official.

Rush paused, but the look in Nora's eye told the tale. She wanted to hear it all—needed to. "Go ahead, Gary."

Gary cleared his throat. "I'm ruling this an accidental

death, but when you look at the report and photos, you'll see some striations on the...on the skull."

"Cause?" Rush asked, his stomach roiling over what Nora might be imagining. He should have taken Gary off speakerphone.

"Unfortunately, they're inconclusive."

"Meaning there could have been foul play involved?" Nora asked, but her voice cracked. "Have you double-checked?"

"I'm sorry, Nora," Gary said. "I have. They could have come from the impact of the car hitting the water, causing her to hit her head on the steering wheel or another part of the vehicle, but I can't be one hundred percent sure."

"Then it's possible that something else caused those marks."

"I don't believe so, no," Gary said, this time a bit firmer. "I think what we have here is a terrible tragedy, and I am sorry for your loss and the loss of your family."

"Thanks, Gary. I appreciate it." Rush hung up before Nora pressed on.

She stood, then sat. Tears spilled over her cheeks as the harsh reality sank in. Rush tried to hold her, but she pushed him away as expected. Instead of getting upset over the fact that she didn't want him or his comfort, he quietly sat while she dealt with the death inwardly, and then she hurried to the bathroom, closing herself off even further from him. When she returned, he stood. "I'm so sorry, Nora Beth. Is there anything I can do?"

"No. She really is gone. Dad will want to have a proper burial. I need to work on the arrangements." She sniffed, wiped her nose on her sleeve and composed herself outwardly. "But I can't dismiss the fact that the striations are inconclusive. That means it's not definite and you know it."

There was no arguing that Gary had been the coroner for over a decade and a doctor for twenty years prior. Nora had latched onto the idea that Marilyn had been hurt that night. Rush massaged the back of his neck, working the tightness out. She had a point, even though it was slight.

"And even if she wasn't murdered, there's money involved. What if she was blackmailed for something—or forbid it all, blackmailing someone— Money laundering, payoffs...the list is endless. Rush, you're a total cop. Tell me you think it's all coincidence and it should be laid to rest and I'll believe you."

He couldn't give her that, as much as he hated to start tearing up innocent families with accusations. "I can't say that. And you know it. I also know you, and you have no plans of laying anything to rest anytime soon. You were pacifying your dad earlier."

"So?"

"So I think it's a good thing he put me next door."

FOUR

Sunday morning had come earlier than Nora would have liked. She'd been sleeping in on Sundays for a while now, but she'd agreed to go to church with her family and she had. First Community Fellowship and its congregation hadn't changed much. Rush had been two rows back with his family—minus Pastor Buchanan—which had been a surprise. Looked like his dad had retired. Nora hadn't kept up with the town news and Dad and Hailey never spoke of Rush. She was thankful for that.

They'd eaten Sunday dinner and now she was bundled up and at the town square for the annual snowman building competition. She'd promised Dalton she'd build one with him. She could count on both hands the years she'd entered this contest with Rush.

Dalton found a good spot next to a bench. "I want to build here."

"Perfect."

"I had a feeling you'd be here today," Rush said with a measure of pep in his voice. "You ran out with your dad pretty fast after the service."

The sermon on the Prodigal Son had unsettled her heart. Truth did that sometimes. She wasn't ready to deal with the messes she'd made trying to be someone she wasn't. "Had to get ready for this." Was he here to baby-sit her? Or... "You building a snowman?"

"No. My sister's kids are." He pointed across the square to his younger sister and her two littles.

"Do you *wanna* build a snowman?" she asked.

"Do you?" His eyebrow slyly arched.

Their gazes held. Memories flooded her mind and trickled all the way down to her tummy. Was he thinking of all their fun in the past? The snowball fights. Hot cocoa and kisses.

"I am." She motioned to the spot she stood on. "With Dalton. We could use some help."

"And how will that look when we whip all the competition, including my niece and nephew? They'll cry for weeks." He chuckled.

"They'll thank you for not helping them. You're terrible at it. Remember the year we built Frosty? You didn't have carrots."

"Hey, the celery worked. Frosty with sinus congestion."

Nora snorted and laughed. "It was gross."

"What? I put a white hanky in his twig hand." Rush's boyish mischief could always melt her like snow on a sunshiny day. "And now I have the urge to build a snowman."

"Then help us and your niece and nephew, but mostly us." She winked.

"Deal."

They began to pack the snow and roll the balls. Rush showed Dalton how to pack it tight and keep it from crumbling as they talked about superheroes and Dalton's enormous Christmas wish list.

"What do you want for Christmas?" Nora asked Rush.

"Easy. Season tickets to the Vols games next year and

worldwide peace. Or I'd settle for you being safe…and at peace."

Nora packed snow on the base of the snowman. "I will be." She caught his eye and held it. Then smacked him with a snowball, launching an all-out war.

"Hey, we're gonna lose if you use up all the snow on each other!" Dalton hollered and broke up the fight. They resumed building.

Nora's toes were cold and some snow had trickled down her collar. She was smoothing out the snowman's midsection when she spotted Len Franklin. He was on the list of people rumored to have been involved with Mom. Rush didn't seem too keen on doing anything but making lists. Nora wanted answers. Fast. Now. "Hey, give me a second," Nora said and darted across the town square, weaving through snowmen, families, friends, couples and benches until she found Len with a middle-aged woman building a snowman.

"Mr. Franklin, I'm Nora Livingstone. Can I talk to you a second?"

Len raised his sunglasses and peered at Nora, his mouth covered with a scarf. "I know who you are, but I don't know why you'd want to talk to me."

She glanced at the woman, who was watching with curiosity. Nora didn't recognize her. Had Len remarried? "It's about my mother, Marilyn, and the rumors surrounding her affair with you."

The woman gasped. "Excuse me," she said in a shrill voice.

A few participants stopped building and gawked.

"And who are you?" Nora asked.

"I'm his wife. And I think I'd know if he'd had an affair. Furthermore, this isn't the time or place to discuss such things."

Nora ignored the woman and felt a hand on her shoulder.

"You're right. This isn't the time or place." Rush had caught her before she had the chance to get answers.

"Was your divorce a result of having an affair with my mother?" Nora asked quieter. "I'm not budging until you tell me the truth."

Len Franklin glanced around and leaned in. "Your mother was a tramp and that's putting it mildly. My divorce had nothing to do with her. And I had nothing to do with her either. I knew better."

The degrading talk stung and Nora's cheeks heated as people whispered, chuckled and gasped.

"Rush, is this how you investigate these days? Sic a weather girl on innocent folks? Don't see you gettin' elected that way." He harrumphed and consoled his second wife.

Rush nearly dragged Nora through the snow and behind one of the store shops. "Have you lost your mind? You can't go off half-cocked like that. Len's wife is from Texas. She never heard the gossip but she'll want answers now, and she may always wonder if there's some truth to that rumor. Do you not understand the definition of discreet? You could have done some real damage, Nora!"

"You mad because I was pushing forward or you might lose a vote for sheriff?"

Rush's jaw dropped, then he narrowed his eyes. "I'm going to pretend you didn't ask me that. Your dad is with Dalton. I'm taking you home before you accuse the entire town of affairs and foul play."

She fell into step with him. Rush was right, though she didn't want to admit it. "I just wanted to get moving on this. We can make lists all day, but until we start asking some questions we've got nothing. And since you haven't said anything, I'm guessing you haven't talked to your dad since last we discussed it."

Rush ignored her and opened the door of his Bronco. "Get in."

She huffed and slid inside.

They didn't speak until they reached her chalet.

Rush cut the engine. "One of us has a badge and one of us doesn't. So, it's my way or I'll make sure you have zero involvement in this at all. I can make that happen, Nora." His tone held no tenderness. He had every right to seethe.

She picked at the edge of her scarf and swallowed a measure of pride. "I'm sorry for what I said. I didn't mean that."

"Fine." Didn't seem the apology was accepted.

They exited the vehicle and Nora stepped inside her chalet. An eerie feeling sent a new wave of chills over her.

"What is it?" Rush asked.

"I don't know." She walked into her bedroom.

The closet door was open. Nora was sure she'd closed it. She tiptoed to the nightstand, heart pounding. What if someone was in the closet now? Without looking, she felt for the gun Rush gave her Friday night. Breath shallow, she frantically searched to no avail.

Glancing down, she saw why.

It was missing.

Rush stood over Nora's nightstand and scanned the bedroom. While it hadn't been tossed, some things did seem to have been moved. The gun missing was the tell-tale sign, but the place was clear. "What do you think he wanted?" Rush asked.

Nora gnawed on her thumbnail. "I don't know. Can't

be the gun. No one would know I had it. I think that was an opportunity he couldn't turn down."

"The only thing I can think of is the photos. He knows something valuable is in that box and he knows you know." Good thing they were at Rush's. "How did he get in?" Rush had searched the chalet and didn't find a forced point of entry.

"The window in the kitchen was unlocked. I didn't realize it until after I got wigged out that someone had been in here. I checked. I should have checked Friday night when I arrived."

No, Rush should have. He'd stayed up late watching the house, making sure she was safe. He'd even spotted the security detail make their thirty-minute cruise by the chalet. With security and Rush being so close, the intruder would have had to have been up in the trees. Watching with binoculars. "I don't like the idea of you being alone in this cabin. Six feet away in another cabin isn't going to be good enough. So before you get all freaked out, I'll stay in the chalet next door. Until midnight. From midnight until seven a.m. I'm bunking on your couch. My car will be next door. No one will think anything untoward is going on, and who's out here to think anything anyway?"

Nora's lips pursed. She didn't love the idea. Rumors were a sore spot, especially if they cast her in a dim light. Nora ran like the wind when trouble came. It was the driving wedge between them. Whether she ran physically or emotionally it was still the same—shutting out Rush. And to say he wasn't doing his job because he wanted votes? That cut deep.

"Okay, Rush. I'll agree to it." She touched his shoulder. "And I really am sorry. I know you'd never ignore your duty. I'm…"

"What?" If she would only open up. What? What would that do besides zero in on his heart and crush it again when she left for Florida?

"Frustrated. That's all."

No, it wasn't. But he didn't push. He didn't want to have to press and push. He'd watched Mama do that with Dad for so long. It did no good. They'd lost Dad to the pain and Rush had lost Nora. He needed to get a handle on that and move on. If he was meant to be a bachelor, he'd deal with it. He only wished the loneliness would go away. But better to be alone than in a marriage that felt one-sided. *God, Mama needs You to marvelously work on her behalf, and so do I.*

"I understand."

"Can I ask you something off topic? It's personal." Nora sucked her lower lip between her teeth. She didn't have to open up but she wanted him to get personal. He almost laughed, but it was far from funny. She didn't even wait for his response. "Where was your dad today? Why isn't he pastoring anymore? How long have you and your family been at First Community Fellowship?"

"That's three questions." And this topic was tender for him. Too tender to get into with a woman who wouldn't reciprocate his feelings. "We've been at FCF for about ten years. Since Dad isn't preaching anymore. He was at home today."

Nora opened her mouth but clamped it closed. "Gonna snow soon. Sleet later tonight."

That wasn't at all what she wanted to say, but relief slid through Rush. He didn't want to discuss Dad. "I know, and the tourists keep pouring in. They may not be able to get out. Tours in the Smokies have been shut down. Too dangerous out there."

Hopefully, it wouldn't slow down business. Tourism

was Splendor Pines' cash cow. Especially during the Christmas season.

"Speaking of dangerous. Do you believe Len Franklin?"

"I don't know." What he did know was he hadn't found any photos that matched a Phantom of the Opera mask with the cuff link. But he had pulled a couple more photos of men in the masks. "I plan to talk to your dad when he gets home. About that money."

He hadn't had the time Saturday, and while he hated doing any kind of business on Sunday, it came with the territory.

"I'll come with you."

"I know you will. I don't want to leave you here alone, but once we get to the house, I want to talk to him by myself. If he is withholding information, it might only be from you. Give me the chance to see if he'll fess up to something to me."

"I owe you that after what I said." The next hour they spent drinking coffee and keeping relatively quiet. "Dad's probably home," she said, staring out the window.

"All right."

Nora grabbed her scarf and coat.

They locked up the chalet and drove to the house. Joshua's car was in the drive. Inside, Joshua sat on the couch watching Dalton put a puzzle together while Hailey was curled up asleep on the love seat. They made small talk, then Rush stood. "Joshua, could we talk privately?"

Joshua set his coffee on the side table and nodded. "My office."

Nora busied herself with Dalton's puzzle. At least she was following through with what she said.

Joshua closed the door to his office and perched on the edge of the desk.

Rush had no easy way of doing this. "We found Marilyn's camera case. Her camera wasn't in it. But two hundred and fifty thousand dollars was." He waited a beat, gauged Joshua's reaction to the news.

Joshua stared past Rush's shoulder, then slowly spoke. "I gave her that for an anniversary gift. Waterproof. She dropped the camera case before that into the lake. She'd cried for days over lost film." Joshua's eyebrows slightly rose and he licked his lips. "You want to know if I was aware that she had that kind of money on her person?"

"Were you?"

"No."

"But you don't seem surprised," Rush said.

Joshua's jaw twitched. "I knew she had a great deal of money. I made weekly deposits into her personal account."

"Why not have a joint account like most married couples?"

Joshua folded his arms over his chest. "We weren't most married couples. Have you ever heard of foster children hoarding food even after they've been adopted into a safe family? Even though they love the new parents and trust them, there's always this fear that they won't get another meal. At some point, they might stop doing it, but until then, they need that feeling of safety. Security."

Rush read between the lines. "You're saying her account was for her to feel secure?" Why would Marilyn feel that way? Had she been a foster kid? "You want to expound further?"

"No. Because it's not pertinent to your investigation. That account was kept open for when or if she returned. You're welcome to the bank records." Joshua opened a filing cabinet and pulled out a manila folder. "She has four thousand dollars in it. It would appear she had been withdrawing money and storing it up, since you found the cash. I can't tell you why." He handed over the information.

"Can't or won't?" Rush asked.

"Marilyn had left before. She didn't stay gone long. I don't know where she went. I think had she not been in an accident, she'd have come back. She loved the girls... and she loved me," he murmured. "I don't care what other people say. I knew her heart."

"Did you argue often?" What man would not confront his wife about rumored affairs—and so many?

"Couples disagree, Rush. Yes, we had arguments. Some were more heated than others."

If Joshua had anything to do with Marilyn's death, Rush would be shocked. He wouldn't rule him out, though. Not yet. Nora believed he was hiding something. Rush wasn't sure it was something sinister, but too many people were keeping things hidden.

FIVE

Rush slid on his hiking boots and tied the laces. At nine o'clock this morning, he'd attended the burial of Marilyn Livingstone, though he'd felt much like an outsider. Only family and a handful of friends had attended. After a small brunch at the main house with immediate family, he'd dropped Nora off at the chalet and went next door to change, and to give her some alone time. She hadn't said much, but she'd shed a few tears.

Between this case, the weather and Nora in general, his mind was muddied. Nora wouldn't let up until she had the answers she wanted. She'd proved that by bombarding Len Franklin, who had called Troy, and Rush had listened to a lecture about keeping her nose out of the investigation. Rush agreed, but clearly, she wouldn't. It would be easier to try to give her some rope and hope she wouldn't hang herself with it. If they worked together, Rush could at least contain her actions, and if things took a turn for the worse he'd be there to protect her.

Rush had filled Nora in on the bank account but he had kept the part about Marilyn's need for security to himself. He'd hoped she'd take this day to be with her family, but he couldn't trust her not to give him the slip and go off on her own. He grabbed his wool coat and faced the treacherous weather. Gray skies. Pregnant with snow. Shivering, he hurried next door to her chalet and knocked.

A few moments later, the door opened and Nora stood in sock feet with a cup of coffee. He wanted to ease into her space, wrap his arms around her and let the warmth seep into him, but those days were over. "Hey," he said instead.

Rush stepped inside and shut the door on the wintry mix coming down. His pillow was resting on the folded-up blanket he'd placed on the end of the sofa earlier this morning before he left.

The cabin smelled of fresh coffee.

Raking her hands through her hair, Nora slurped her java—didn't look to be her first—as the gales blasted against the chalet rattling the windows and whistling down the chimney flue. The fire inside popped and flickered. Snow blew from the bare branches and ice crusted the windowpanes and porch railing.

"I've been studying weather satellites online, tracking the storm heading our way. A foot of snow in the past three days and an inch of ice."

"Is that all you've been doing?" he asked and poked his nose over her shoulder. *The Old Farmer's Almanac* was open in another tab. "Don't you want a day to mourn?"

"This is my way," she said quietly and set her mug on the wooden table. "I've been looking into the weather from seventeen years ago. But there's not much to go on. No data for snow depth. Zero inches recorded for rainfall. Mean wind speed had only been four miles per hour. Maximum was seventeen. Not bad enough to knock someone off the road and especially not if the roads weren't slick with water or ice."

Rush gave his head a small shake. She might as well be speaking a foreign language. Nora had been infatuated with the weather since as long as he'd known her. Once they'd sneaked out of school their sophomore year to chase a tornado. They'd nearly died. Definitely got grounded. But there wasn't much Rush wouldn't have done for or with Nora.

"Why isn't there much to go on?"

"All weather information is collected by the National Climatic Data Center, but only what's reported. Not every station reports every day—or at all."

Nora continued to study weather satellite images and maps, jotting down notes while Rush made a cup of coffee.

She popped up from the screen. "Do you want some coffee?"

He held up his mug and winked.

A fresh flood of pink filled her cheeks. "I can get lost in research sometimes."

"You don't say."

She closed down her laptop, then poured another cup from the pot. Steam billowed into her face. "I know you're not simply here for coffee."

"I'm not." He set his cup on the table. "I'm going to talk to Ward McKay. He's renovating the hotel over on Route 5."

"I want to go."

He folded his arms over his chest. "I knew you'd say that. Which is why I'm going unofficially."

Nora frowned, then slid her glance over him and blushed. He swallowed hard. Nora may have been aiming for stoicism, but he'd recognized approval in her once-over—attraction. "What?" he asked, forcing her to either lie or tell him she was checking him out.

"I noticed you're dressed casually. No uniform."

Half-truth.

He spread his arms out. "I don't work all the time."

"Have a life, do ya?"

No. Not really. "Do you?"

"It's on hold at the moment until I hear from Florida."

"What if you don't hear from them? Then what are you going to do?" Would it ever appeal to her to stay?

"I have a few irons in the fire."

"Any around these parts?" he asked as nonchalantly as possible.

"No. I'm ready to branch out of Tennessee. See new things." Since when? "Let me change and we can be on our way." Nora hurried to her bedroom and fifteen minutes later entered the living room dressed in jeans that were tucked into knee-high black boots that matched her sweater with a droopy-looking collar. "What's wrong? You're staring at me."

"Nothing." It was hard to focus when the prettiest woman he'd ever seen was standing two feet away smelling like an orchard. "But before we go, just because I'm going unofficially doesn't mean you have free rein. I'm asking the questions and I'm going to be discreet."

She saluted him and slid her knit cap on her head. "Aye aye, *mon capitaine*." Brushing past him, she stepped onto the porch and took a step, slipping.

Rush scrambled and caught her around the waist before her backside met the wooden stair. She turned in his arms, her breath pluming between them, cheeks rosy. She blinked a few times, not hurrying from his arms. And he hadn't let go either.

A beat passed.

Two.

"You okay?" he asked, hoping his tone hadn't revealed his feelings. Having her in his arms, so close. So soft. It had unleashed a storm inside him.

"Yeah," she said with a faint voice. "Good thing you're here."

He brushed away a hair that had stuck to her lip gloss. "Guess so." Righting her, he led her to his truck parked at his chalet and opened the door for her. Once she was inside, he jumped in the driver's seat and cranked the engine. Christmas oldies blared from the radio and he adjusted the volume.

"You really do love jamming to Christmas music," she said.

"Can't a guy like Christmas?"

"Not if the guy won't even put up a Christmas tree." Rush had always loved Christmas as much as Nora. And here they both were without the festive spirit in the form of a blue spruce or Douglas fir.

"Touché." They made small talk until they reached the Evergreen Hotel.

"You didn't mention it was the Parkwells' hotel." Parkwells. Ainsley's family. He hadn't actually thought about it until now.

Tension in the air swirled over the name.

"Nora, that was a long time ago." Rush swiveled in his seat to face her. "I can only apologize so many times for not revealing I was dating Ainsley. But when we're together—I mean when we used to be together—it's like the rest of the world didn't exist. It was just you and me. I got caught up in that."

Nora looked away, then faced him. "I believe you, Rush. But I can't forget what happened, and I'm going to feel awkward around Ainsley. I can't help it."

Rush understood. "If it makes you feel any better, she won't be here. She only worked for her dad while she was in school. She's a guidance counselor for the middle and high school. Kids won't be out for a few more days."

"Okay."

"And thank you. For believing me."

She nodded.

"Now let's go see Ward McKay and hope he'll give us some information."

They hurried to the main doors and entered, shutting out the biting cold. Some of the walls were charred. Destroyed.

"What happened?" Nora asked.

"Fire last month. Bad wiring. It'll be summer before they can reopen."

The sound of hammers, drills and shuffling about drew their attention past the elevators and down one of the first-floor halls. "Parkwell can't seem to catch a break," Rush muttered as they stepped over heavy plastic, where painting crews had been working.

"What do you mean?" Nora asked.

He should have kept his mutter quiet. Ainsley had confided in him while they were dating that her father seemed to fall into bad investments and had been pretty stressed out. It was straining her parents' marriage. But then he'd bought this small hotel and things seemed to look up. Now a fire.

"Just, he hasn't been the star of the show when it comes to business deals." He nonchalantly shrugged and kept moving. Construction crew members passed by and he stopped one. "Hey, you seen Ward?"

"Second floor," one mumbled, and hauled some lumber on his shoulder into another room. "Use the stairs. Elevators aren't working right now."

"Thanks." At the end of the hall, the stairwell door was already open and they climbed the flight of stairs that led to the second floor. More noisy construction was going on up here along with some classic rock music.

Rush and Nora wandered the hall until Rush spotted Ward. Guy had been a legend on the football field—played some college ball for the Vols. But like most people, he made his way back home. Unlike Nora, who wanted nothing more than to stay gone. Being here seemed almost painful for her and not only because of the memories of her mother. Something more was going on but she refused to confide in Rush. And he couldn't push. He was keeping the kiss between the mystery man and Marilyn to himself.

Nora didn't trust him with her feelings. Rush couldn't trust her with this. She'd already proved she wasn't going to be discreet. If she found out about what Rush had seen, she'd go vigilante and ignore others' feelings. Might even falsely accuse someone. And that's another reason he'd let her come along. To test her with Ward. If she could be discreet and not hotheaded this time, he'd reveal the truth. Overly cautious was better than hurting and wrecking innocent lives.

"Hey, Ward," Rush said.

"Were you having an affair with my mom and if so, did you have anything to do with her death?" Nora asked.

So much for trust and discretion.

Heat filled Nora's cheeks as Rush's sight bored into the side of her head. Okay, she'd been blunt, but she was losing time. Florida could call any minute and she'd be leaving. And if she did, no one would put in the time or effort like herself.

Ward McKay slowly removed his construction hat and eyed her with a mix of regret and heat. "Hello to you too, Nora."

Rush needled her lower back and stepped in front of her. "Sorry, Ward."

Sorry? This man could be a murderer. She could have used more tact, sure, but apologizing? Not in a million years.

Ward ran his hand through his thick salt-and-pepper hair. "I figured you'd eventually come calling about Marilyn. Didn't realize you deputized her daughter."

Rush shot Nora a glare. "I didn't. We're here unofficially."

Eyeing Nora, Ward grunted. "Doesn't feel unofficial."

Nora couldn't keep silent. "Official. Unofficial. Either way, you might have some answers. Did you have an affair with my mother?"

Ward studied his feet, then looked at Nora. He tossed out his hands. "What do you want me to say? I'm sorry? Because I am, but I wasn't then."

His words punched her straight in the stomach. She nearly bowled over from the blow. For the first time ever, she heard the truth from someone who had no reason to lie.

Rush lightly touched her upper back.

"Did my father know?" she choked out. There was no denying it anymore.

Ward licked his lower lip and jammed his hands into his pockets. "I never told him. Doubtful Mari did."

"Marilyn. Her name was Marilyn." How dare he use a pet name for her mother in front of her! Where was the respect?

He turned to Rush. "I suspect that Joshua has an idea. He's never approached me, though."

"How long was the affair?" Rush asked.

"A year."

A whole year? Nora couldn't breathe. This was a bad idea. Maybe she should have listened to Rush. She wasn't as prepared to hear these things as she thought.

"Did you see her the night she died?" Rush asked.

"I did. But we were over by then. She called things off." His tone held sorrow and even regret. The man had genuinely been in love with her mother! He pulled his phone from his pocket, checked it and texted. "Sorry. Work stuff."

"Did the affair contribute to your divorce and family leaving town?" Rush slightly cringed as if asking the question hurt.

"Most definitely." He paused. "Nora, I really would rather not discuss this in front of you."

"If you're embarrassed, that's on you, Ward." She wouldn't give him an ounce of easy.

"I'm not. I don't want *you* to have to hear this."

"You weren't thinking about me then! Why think about me now?" Venom dripped from her words, all the hurt and anger. She couldn't stop it if she wanted to. "You hurt so many people! How could you?" Unwanted tears sprang in her eyes.

Rush faced Nora, his back to Ward, and he gently put his hands on her shoulders, leaning close and lowering his voice. "Why don't you go wash your face. Take a few moments. I'll finish this up and tell you everything you want or need to know."

As much as she hated it, she needed to pull it together. "Fine," she said reluctantly.

"Bathroom on the second floor isn't working. Use the one on the first. Down the hall from the pool. Under construction but in working order," Ward offered. "I'm sorry, Nora."

"Save it, Ward." She stomped from the hotel room and down the hall to the stairwell. On the first floor, she turned right, the cold draft seeping through her thick gray peacoat. Securing her scarf tighter around her neck, she passed plastic-covered walls and doors. The hard truth had left her exposed and vulnerable. She couldn't stop imagining Ward and her mother as a couple. Her father all alone. Those images turned her stomach.

Rush had warned her.

She hadn't listened.

Hammering and drilling echoed through the lonely, dark hall. Metal burning turned up her nose.

Bathroom. Covered in the same heavy Visqueen.

She shoved it aside, the rattling noise sending her insides kangarooing. Bending, she checked for feet under the stalls. She went to the mirror, ran water and waited on it to warm.

She closed her eyes, splashed water on her face.

Suddenly she was yanked away from the faucet, a strong grip on her coat collar. Through the mirror, a burly man's partially covered face stared back. He wore a construction hat and a painter's mask.

Nowhere to run.

Swinging her purse, she caught him on the shoulder but it didn't stop him. He slammed her back against the wall by the bathroom door.

Heart pounding, she dug her nails into his hands that were clutching her throat.

"You don't listen! You must have a death wish."

Snatching the hanging Visqueen from the door, he ripped it as she kicked and swung, but his grip around her throat was a force, and his hands were like vises. Nora let out a strangled cry as he draped the plastic like a tight blanket across her face.

Can't breathe!

Panic set in. Blood pounded in her temples.

Pop!

Pop!

Had he shot her?

She couldn't see. Every time she inhaled, plastic entered her mouth, the taste dirty and bitter.

God, help me! He'd yanked the thick material across her face and nail-gunned it to the wall, trapping her to suffocate! The last thing she heard was him laughing.

Nora couldn't tear through it. Too thick.

Couldn't get oxygen.

Couldn't calm down. Hysteria was taking over. With each scream, she inhaled the plastic.

No air. Spots formed. Sweat slicked her temples and back as she clawed at the plastic.

She was passing out.

"Nora! You down here?" Rush called out. "Hey, I don't want to come in, but I will if you don't say something."

Barely any energy left, she forced her arm out the door and waved.

See my arm. See I need help.

"Nora!"

In a flash, the sound of ripping came through the suffocating barrier, and a blast of wonderful oxygen filled her lungs; she gulped it in. Rush held her up. "Did you see him?"

She shook her head, coughing and inhaling deep breaths. "Keep this." He handed her the knife he'd used to cut away the plastic.

Rush shot from the bathroom and she slid down the wall, pushing back her sweaty, matted hair. She could have died.

It felt like an eternity before Rush returned and knelt in front of her. "What happened?"

She told him through ragged breaths. "If you hadn't shown up…"

He drew her to him and stroked her hair. "You said he

wore a hard hat and had a nail gun." He looked around the bathroom, at the tools lying on the floor. "He must have taken it with him. I don't see either."

"Do you think he's working here or he followed us?" The thought froze her blood in her veins.

Rush frowned. "I can't say for sure. Either scenario is plausible, but I didn't notice anyone following us on the way here. Seems likely he's an employee. I'll get a list from Ward."

"You're going to interrogate a whole construction crew?"

"Just the ones who clocked in." He caressed her cheek. "You sure you're okay?"

She nodded. "How many do you think are here?"

"Thirty, maybe fifty. I don't know."

"That's going to take a lot of time." Time they didn't have.

Rush gripped her shoulders. "I don't care if it takes me till Kingdom Come. Whoever did this isn't going to get away with it."

His sober tone slid into her, melting away the fear until it waved again. "Rush, he wasn't trying to scare or threaten me. He wanted me dead." Tears stung the backs of her eyes. "He's going to strike again."

"I'm going to protect you, Nora Beth. I promise." Cupping her cheek, he forced her to make eye contact, to see he would do whatever it took to keep her safe. "Tell me you trust me."

He wasn't asking her to trust him with her heart. Just her life. "I trust you. To keep me safe."

"It's a start," he muttered. "I don't want you here any longer than you have to be. I'll get you back to Pine Refuge and I want you stuck to your daddy like glue, understand?"

Nora nodded and Rush escorted her outside and into the Bronco. He started the engine and blasted the heat; it blew cold so he turned it back down until it warmed. "Do you still want to keep looking into the past? I plan to continue investigating these attacks, but we don't have to pursue the past."

"Depends. You believe foul play was involved that night?" She didn't want to have to convince Rush that something sinister happened to Mom. She wanted Rush to believe it for himself. If he did, he'd work harder, be more aggressive in the investigation.

"We can't prove it. The striations on her skull are inconclusive. Even if you find the weather in all likelihood didn't cause the accident, there are a million other things that could have sent her into the lake. Deer. Bobcat. Dog. Not paying attention…"

She got it. The list was endless. "We can't prove anything. But if we keep poking around, someone will eventually tell us something or lead us somewhere. And we know the report is inconclusive, but no one else knows. We have leverage."

"Nora," he groaned.

"It's not illegal to bend the truth. It's not even entrapment. I've watched every legal show on the planet. I can google it and I will." She pulled her phone from her purse.

Rush chuckled. "Okay, Detective Livingstone. I see what you're saying. I don't like it, though."

"Of course you don't. But you have nothing to lose."

He gripped the wheel and his jaw ticked. Had she struck some kind of nerve?

Turning the heat full blast, he murmured, "Some of us already lost everything because of this."

Was he talking about losing her? What else could

he mean? What could she say? Sorry didn't seem good enough for how much she'd hurt Rush.

Rush changed the subject. "Do you want the lowdown on Ward?"

"Yeah. I wanna know." Better to keep it from getting personal anyway.

"He thinks your mom was involved with someone else besides him—toward the end of their relationship."

Nora covered her face. The overwhelming humiliation set her cheeks aflame. What in the world was wrong with that woman? What if she'd passed down the cheating genes? Was that even possible?

"Nora," he said softly. "Do you want me to go on?"

She wanted a time machine to go back, change everything. "Go on. I'm fine."

"He fell in love with her, Nora. Wanted to marry her. Told his wife. It broke up their home but your mom wouldn't leave your dad."

Nora snorted. "What in the world was keeping her?"

"I don't know. I suspect your dad knew. I have no clue why he wouldn't give her the boot." His cheeks flushed. "Sorry."

"No, he'd have every right. How many times can one betray you until you walk away? How could he have trusted her? Yet he says he continued to put money in a personal account. I'd have put a tracking chip under her skin or something." Nora half laughed. What wasn't her dad telling her? Why would a woman not leave? Why would a man hang on?

"I think Ward's still angry over their breakup, but I'm guessing. And that doesn't mean he did anything that night."

"But so far he's our best suspect. Unless your dad

knows something." She waited for Rush to respond, but his nostrils flared and he sighed.

"I said I would. I will."

"Today."

"Today. Now. Do you want to hear the rest of my conversation with Ward?"

She nodded.

"He said she visited a bar and grill outside of town. Mac's? Sound familiar?"

"I mean, I've heard of it but I've never been."

"He suspects she was meeting a man there. It's what caused the downward turn in their affair. Ward doesn't know who the man might be. Never saw her with anyone else during their time together."

"I guess we need to take a trip to Mac's after you get that list of construction workers from Ward."

Nora wasn't ready for what they might find. But she had no other options.

SIX

Rush glanced out his office window into the bull pen, where desks butted up against one another.

He'd nearly lost Nora this morning.

The memory sent a new wave of sickness into his stomach.

After he'd dropped her off at her dad's, he got the list from Ward McKay, went back to the site and did interviews through lunch. Fifty-two men and not one claimed to have done it. He hadn't expected them to. But it was still possible that they'd been followed or a worker not on that list had shown up. No one would have thought anything about him being on-site.

Rush had checked in by phone with Nora after lunch. She'd been searching weather maps and online sites to try to discover the weather that night along with helping her sister at the guest center.

Now it was nearly five thirty and he was hungry, but every time he pictured Nora with plastic nail-gunned across her face, he lost his appetite. He picked up his cell phone and called as he gathered his coat and keys. She answered on the second ring.

"Any news?" she asked.

"No. But we'll keep searching. Have you eaten?"

"Not since lunch. You?" Her tone had a hint of hopefulness.

"How about I stop by Rudy's and grab some Italian food and we can eat in. The weather is—"

"Going to get nastier around eight. Sounds good. I'm at the chalet with Dad."

"Okay. He going to eat with us?"

"No."

"Chicken Parm still your favorite?"

A beat of silence passed through the line. "Yeah. Yeah it is." Was that surprise he detected? There wasn't anything about her he'd forgotten. Not even the fact that she loved Christmas but hadn't put a tree up since her mother died. Now she'd been attacked multiple times and heard straight from the horse's mouth that her mother had been involved in several affairs.

"It'll be about an hour before I can get to you. That okay?"

"Sure. I'll be the one with the growling stomach."

He caught her humor but didn't miss the grief beneath it. "Sit tight, Nora Beth." By the time she fell asleep tonight, he might be able to make it a little better.

Sheriff Parsons met Rush at the main doors. "You callin' it a night, Rush?"

"Yeah. No news on the Livingstone case. You hear anything new?" Rush asked as they pressed into the frigid night, light snow but heavy, dry wind. Later, it was supposed to snow and ice again.

"Nope. How are things?" He gave Rush the inquisitive eye.

"With Nora?"

Troy chuckled. "Yes, with Nora. She's a sweet girl, son. But I don't see her sticking around long. Don't get too tied up."

He wouldn't.

What he was about to do had nothing to do with personal feelings; it was about making a friend feel better—or trying to. "We're friends. Which is more than we used to be. I'll take it."

Troy clapped Rush's shoulder. "All right, Rush. All right." He climbed in his truck and pulled away as Rush slid into his Bronco and headed for his parents' house.

Inside, his mother sat on the couch knitting a pink-and-gray scarf. "Rush, what are you doing here?"

"Can't a guy come by and see his mama?" He bent and kissed her cheek. "I smell cookies."

She snickered. "Family will be here tomorrow. Wanted to get a jump start on snacks. But help yourself to some and take a few to Nora." She looked up at him. "How is she?"

"Worse for the wear, but truckin' on."

Dad stepped out of the hallway in his navy blue robe and moccasin slippers. "Nora home?" he asked.

He'd aged dramatically in the last decade. Frail. His hair, once dark blond like Rush's, now full of gray. "Yeah, she's home. Helping look into her mom's disappearance."

Dad's mouth pinched and divots formed between his eyebrows, but he offered nothing. Rush expected no less. Nora didn't understand who Dad was these days.

He turned to Mom. "Do you still have those extra boxes of ornaments up in the attic and the tree you used to put in the family room?"

She squinted. "I believe so. You putting up a tree?"

"That's my plan." At Nora's. Who would press him about if he'd questioned Dad or not. He'd promised. "Dad, while I'm thinking about it, do you remember anyone in particular wearing a Phantom of the Opera mask the night Marilyn went missing or anything that might be helpful for me in this investigation?"

"Can't say," he grumbled, and shuffled into the kitchen. *Can't or wouldn't?*

A few moments later, he heard the cookie jar lid clinking. Rush sighed and climbed up into the attic, retrieving two huge boxes of ornaments, and then he brought down the tree. Christmas tree lots wouldn't be open this late. Artificial would have to do.

Fifteen minutes later, he was back on the road. Snow steadily coming down. The curves were rough to handle and slick, but he made it to Rudy's and then to Nora's chalet over an hour later. Living room lights glowed. Smoke puffed from the chimney.

He grabbed the to-go boxes and made it to her door, slipping only once. He knocked with his boot. "It's me, Nora Beth."

The door opened. "I'm starving."

"You're welcome." He stepped inside and greeted Joshua before he left. Rush locked the door behind him. The cabin quickly filled with Italian spices, onion and garlic. Nora had already set the table.

"Thank you for dinner."

He handed her the chicken Parm and piled the linguine on his plate. They made small talk while they wolfed down their meals and he gave her a brief update on the interviews and that his dad had no information to offer, but he didn't want to talk shop tonight.

"You want hot cocoa?" she asked.

"Actually, I was thinking about something else."

Nora's sculpted eyebrow rose.

Rush chuckled. "It's outside." He stood. "Be back." He braved the cold and brought in the two boxes.

"What in the world?" Nora said and retrieved the top box. "More pictures?"

"No. For the rest of the night, I kinda don't want to talk about the case." Rush set the box on the floor, then went back out and brought in the tree.

"Rush, what is going on?" she asked, confusion filling her face.

He plopped the tree box down and dusted his hands on his pants. "You've had a horrible day. And I thought maybe we could bring back some good times tonight." He paused, hoping this would be okay with her. "It's time to start putting a tree up, Nora Beth," he whispered.

She scanned the tree box and ornaments and shook her head. "I don't think I can."

"Yes, you can. You've pushed this case and been attacked but you keep going." If there was a time to tuck tail, this was it. But she hadn't. It shifted something inside him. "You can put this tree up. Remember the good times. Believe there will be more to come." He leaned down to catch her eye. "Let's do it together."

Nora gnawed her bottom lip and crossed her arms across her chest, her oversize red sweater swallowing her in a way that made her ridiculously appealing. She nodded. "Okay, Rush. You're right. I need some kind of goodness to end this night."

Rush's chest swelled with satisfaction and a Psalm came to mind. "'I had fainted, unless I had believed to see the goodness of the Lord in the land of the living,'" he quoted. "We'll see the goodness of the Lord in all this. I believe it."

Nora opened a box. "I'm glad you do, Rush. You've always had stronger faith than me." She hauled out glass ornaments in red, gold, green and silver.

Rush pulled out the three-piece prelit tree. He put the

sections together, plugged it in and hoped the lights all worked. "I think your faith was pretty strong until that night." He and Nora had shared that—faith. Hope in the Lord.

He still hoped. Still believed, but sometimes he had doubts. When it came to finding a wife, having a family. He had to admit he'd been struggling to trust God in that area.

"It's too quiet in here," she said, and grabbed her cell phone. She set it on a small docking station on the counter and a Christmas music station belted from the speaker. "Rockin' Around the Christmas Tree" played, bringing the atmosphere back to an upbeat vibe. A few lights were out and he messed around until he got them working.

"You ready?"

Nora stared at the white lights casting a romantic glow on the cabin. Her eyes filled with moisture, and Rush couldn't help it; he closed the distance between them and laced his hand in hers.

"I forgot how much I've missed this. Mom used to say colored lights were fun, but white lights were pure. Innocent. Clean. She was right."

Rush studied the lights. He'd never thought about it that way. In terms of innocent. Clean. Interesting for a woman who had multiple affairs. Something stirred deep within him. He couldn't put a finger on it, but all of a sudden, he felt sorry for Marilyn Livingstone.

Nora started trimming the tree with the glass ornaments and humming along with the music as "Blue Christmas" belted through the room. He'd had some pretty blue Christmases over the past several years.

"What are you asking Santa for this year?" He placed a gold glittery ornament on the tree.

"You know what I want, but since we aren't discussing

that right now…a job would be pretty great. Bills won't pay themselves." She dug through the ornaments and retrieved a small wooden box. "What's this?"

"Oh, wow." Rush laughed, but his chest tightened. "Open it."

She did. Her eyes widened and she gaped. "I can't believe you still have this." Nora held up a ceramic hand, painted red and white like a candy cane. She held her own hand against it. Perfect fit.

Ought to be. It was hers.

She snickered until she found the acrylic painted inscription written on the palm, then she sobered. "Do… do you want me to put it back? Or…"

"Hang it," he managed, emotion choking his voice. "It was a good memory."

"You have the other three?" she asked.

"Somewhere." He turned away to get his bearings. She'd made that first hand in their freshman year of high school. The plan was to make one each year forever. And one day when they were old, their tree would be nothing but Christmas hands.

He read the black painted note.

You have my hand and my heart. Forever. I love you always.
Nora

The date was right under her name. Over twenty years ago.

He didn't have her hand. Or her heart.

"Silent Night" came on the music station. His favorite. Perfect song to match the atmosphere outside, where fat wet flakes fell. It was a winter wonderland.

The fire inside crackled.

Nora's candle smelled wonderful. Not as good as her, though.

"You want cocoa now?" Nora asked softly.

"Sure."

He continued hanging ornaments. At the bottom of the decorations, he found three more wooden boxes but he couldn't bring himself to open them, read the inscriptions or to hang them on the tree. "I'm gonna take these empty boxes out to the Bronco."

Without wasting time, he hurried outside and put them in the back of the truck. When he returned inside, Nora sat on the sofa, feet curled up underneath her as she watched the lights on the tree. By the firelight, she was breathtaking.

A smile tugged at her lips.

She was deep into memories. Fond ones. Which was what he wanted from the start. He wondered if any of those memories included him. The teakettle whistled and he motioned for her to stay put. "I got it."

"I put the cocoa mix in the mugs already."

He poured the water into the mugs—not his favorite kind of cocoa but it would do in a pinch. He stirred them and brought them to the couch, sitting beside her.

Nora wrapped her slender fingers around her mug and inhaled.

Curiosity got the best of him. "What were you thinking about just now?"

Nora's face glowed against the flames of the fireplace. "When I was little, Dad always let me put the angel on the tree. He'd say, 'Nora, you're my sweetheart.' But I haven't been a sweetheart. I left him when he needed me most. Left Hailey…" Shifting, she faced him. "You…" she whispered. "Sometimes I wonder what would have happened if I hadn't pulled away from you after Mom vanished."

Rush knew exactly what would have happened.

He'd have married her.

Nora peered into Rush's warm brown eyes, not sure what she hoped to see or hear from his mouth. They couldn't go back. Couldn't change the past, but he brought back her best Christmas memories with her family—decorating the tree by the fireside and drinking hot cocoa while listening to festive music. He did it because that's who he was. Compassionate, selfless and generous. He was going the extra mile to see to her safety, knowing he might be in jeopardy too. Not to mention, he probably had a life but he'd put it on hold—for her.

Seeing that ceramic hand had only brought back memories of two teenagers dreaming of a future together, when it seemed bright and full of hope, when it was like the white lights. Innocent. Pure. Untainted by mistakes, scandals and Nora's insecurities.

Rush ran his hand through her hair, brushing it from her face. "I wonder sometimes too." He held her eyes captive as the wind howled and rattled the windowpanes. The smell of chocolate on his breath reached her as he slowly descended on her lips. "I think we would have made a great life, Nora Beth."

Would they have? Would Mom's scandals have hung over them like ice-encased branches, shattering over their happy homemade lives? Would Rush have gotten bored with Nora and cheated? Would Nora have cheated on him?

As his lips met hers, scraping on the roof drew her attention away. She drew back, almost thankful for the distraction. "What was that?"

Rush glanced up. "Probably tree branches." When he met her eyes, he sighed. "If you weren't okay with where this was going, Nora, you could have said so."

She wasn't using the noise to stop the intended kiss. Prickles ran along her skin. "I wasn't, but…we can't let the way we felt about each other in the past trip us up now. We're…we've been over a long time, Rush."

"Is this about what happened with Ainsley?"

"No." Maybe. Partly. "I'm leaving after Christmas. I can't stay here permanently. I don't want to. And I don't see you ever leaving. That kinda puts a halt on anything between us, don't you think?"

"I think—"

Crack!

"Get down," Rush hollered, and shoved Nora on the floor between the couch and the coffee table.

"Was that a gunshot?"

Rush drew his gun and crouched low, moving toward the window in the breakfast area. Nora curled into a fetal position watching, waiting.

Metal outside clanged. Rush turned the knob on the door. "Don't move. I'll be back."

Panic raced through her system. "Don't! Rush, you could get shot!"

He placed his index finger on his lips and slipped out the back door. She threw up a prayer that God would keep Rush safe.

Scraping on the roof continued. Snow fell like curtains of cotton blocking her view into the woods. She couldn't huddle like a scared rabbit and do nothing! Not when Rush was out there risking his life to keep her safe. Crawling across the living room, she made her way to the back door. The only weapon in her possession had been stolen. She was defenseless against someone with a gun, but Rush could be hurt—could use another pair of eyes at least. As she reached for the knob, the door swung open and a blast of cold air swirled with snow into the kitchen area.

Nora yelped, then realized it was Rush.

"What are you doing?" he demanded.

"I was coming to help you. Is he out there?" she asked and balled her fist to hide her trembling hand.

Rush eased her up to her feet, his nose and cheeks pink, hands icy. He'd hurried out without a coat. "A tree split on the north side of the house. Barely missed the roof. Sounded like a gunshot. But there are footprints out there. Fairly large. Work boots, possibly." He rubbed his upper arms. "I think the tree splitting scared him off, and he knocked over the garbage can. Must have been crouching behind it."

Lurking.

Nora shivered.

Rush led her to the fireplace and they sat on the hearth; he might be warming up cold bones from the weather, but no amount of heat could warm up the fear racing through Nora's.

"I followed the footprints into the woods, but without a flashlight it's useless. And with the snow coming down this hard, they'll be covered by the time I can get back out there," Rush said.

Nora rubbed her clammy hands together. "So the rustling on the roof actually was ice weighing down branches and dragging with the wind?"

He held his hands, palms open to the fire. "I suspect."

A gust of wind shook the door and whistled in the flue. The lights flickered. Ice, most likely, was encrusting power lines. Whoever was spying must be desperate to come out in this kind of weather. "If he was in work boots, could it be the same attacker from the hotel?"

"I don't know." Rush frowned. "When you're at work, do you keep your cell phone on to hear notifications?"

Where was this going? "Depends. If I don't mind interruptions, then yeah, I keep it on. Why?"

"It just hit me. Earlier when Ward got that text... I didn't hear it. Not even a buzz. The place was loud and noisy. Wouldn't he have it on to hear the ding?"

Nora's mind raced. "He checked it, then sent a text... Do you think he faked getting a text so he could send one to whoever attacked me? Let him know where I was? What better alibi than the Chief Deputy?"

"We come in and Ward knows what we're after. But that also means he's not working alone—if this speculation is correct."

At least this time, Rush didn't apologize for it. But the thought of more than one killer after her—a band or at the very least a pair of killers working in tandem—terrified her. "If he is working with an employee, then we can't rely on the list he gave us. He could have easily had his accomplice's name removed."

"Valid point. If it's an employee. We don't know anything concrete, so it's not like I can subpoena his phone records, texts." Rush faced the flames, eyes appearing even darker against the firelight. "His information on Marilyn meeting someone at the grill might be a rabbit trail."

"Best way to find out is to go to Mac's tomorrow and hope the owner can tell us something—or the manager if he or she still works there," Nora said. The lights dimmed, flickered and went out, leaving them with only the firelight and the candle she'd purchased earlier.

"Extra candles?" Rush asked.

"I think I saw some tea lights in the nightstand drawer." She used her cell phone flashlight to guide her into the bedroom. Retrieving the box of tea lights and a lighter, she lit them and scattered them throughout the house. In the living room, Rush peeped out the windows.

"Lights are on at the main house and lodge," he said.

"Generator. Chalets and cabins don't have them. I imagine Guest Services will be getting a boatload of calls tonight."

Rush's cell phone rang.

"Hey, Troy," he said. His face grew stern. "Okay, I'll be there as quick as I can." He listened a few moments more, then hung up. "I need to take you up to the main house. Car accident on Route 5. Doesn't look good."

Nora's stomach knotted. "What if he comes back? To the main house?"

Rush laid gentle hands on her shoulders. "I can't say for certain, but I think you'll be safe. Between me chasing him off and the weather…"

But he couldn't say for sure.

"Can I come with you? I'll stay in the car. Promise."

Rush rubbed his earlobe—telltale sign he was thinking about it. "The weather is terrible. Let me take you to your father. I'll come back for you. Three hours tops."

"Okay." She slipped into her coat and Rush's Bronco, then called her dad to let him know she was coming home.

Rush walked her inside and squeezed her hand. He seemed to want to say something more, but instead he motioned a hand to the door.

"Lock this behind me. I'll call you when I'm on my way back."

She simply nodded and closed the door. Dad stood just inside the foyer in his robe and slippers. The backup generator had kept the lights on and the fridge humming. "Everything okay, hon?"

"Yeah. Wreck on Route 5. Rush had to go." She left out the scare from earlier. "Hailey here?"

"No, she's up at the lodge. I was going to head that way too, but Dalton's asleep."

"I can keep an eye on him."

"And who will keep an eye on you?"

Point taken. "I'm going to go lie down." She kissed Dad's cheek and retired to her old bedroom, but sleep wouldn't come. An hour later, she tiptoed downstairs for a cup of warm milk. The greenery on the banister poked at her fingers. Hailey had decorated in silver and gold with pops of red. Festive. Elegant. From the kitchen, she studied the tree. White lights like Mom loved. Childhood ornaments along with glass ornaments. Gold ribbon cascaded down the ten-foot tree. Stockings hung on the mantel. Four. Hailey, Nora, Dalton and Dad.

Dad dozed in the recliner, lightly snoring.

She'd rifled through the offices in the lodge, but she never searched Dad's home office. Tight-lipped meant keeping something hidden. He might be hiding it in his office. Hurrying quietly down the hall, she slipped into Dad's office and closed the door. The lamplight cast a soft glow over the dark wood. A sliver of guilt niggled at her, but she ignored it.

She rummaged through drawers and filing cabinets. Nothing that raised red flags or held secrets. Could his lack of words and pressing an investigation simply be the way he grieved? Privately? He might be able to let things go, but Nora couldn't, especially after Ward McKay's outright admission of guilt. It had lodged like a wet clump of dough in her stomach and grew until she couldn't find a single drop of peace, but only more questions.

Questions that wouldn't be answered here.

On her way to the door, she tripped over the area rug, peeling it back to reveal a small exposed bump in the hardwood. Had his flooring been warped? Kneeling to toss back the rug and leave everything as it was, she noticed the board wasn't uneven, it was raised. Using her thumbs, she pushed the board out of the groove and two more came loose. Underneath lay a small fire safe.

Her heart raced and she quickly pulled the safe from the floor.

No key. She hadn't seen a key while searching the drawers and cabinets.

Dad's set hung in the kitchen. Nora put everything back the way it was and carried the fire safe to her room, hiding it before going back down to retrieve Dad's keys.

He still snoozed in the recliner. She spotted them hanging on the hook by the back door. Without causing too much jingle, she gripped them and raced upstairs, then locked the door.

Chest pounding, she flipped through the keys until she found a small silver one.

It was now or never. She might find nothing but money and valuables, but at least she'd know.

She opened the safe.

Inside was a box lying on one lone manila file folder. She opened the box. Several legal papers were sandwiched inside; she scanned them and gasped.

Her blood ran cold.

SEVEN

Nora's eyes blurred with tears, as a pain, deep and raw, cut like a jagged blade through her heart. Dad had definitely been hiding something.

Like the fact that Nora wasn't his biological daughter.

Whose daughter was she? She could hardly breathe as she blinked away the tears and scanned the documents.

One stood out. A legal agreement.

This hereby states that Scott M. Rhodes relinquishes all parental rights for Nora Jane Cotter.

Cotter—her mother's maiden name.

Scott Rhodes.

Who was this man who fathered her but didn't want a single thing to do with her? She read on and gaped. No. This wasn't true. Couldn't be.

The only dad she'd ever known had paid Scott Rhodes half a million dollars and had agreed to pay him one hundred thousand dollars a year for the rest of Scott's natural life.

So that's what it cost to give her away.

Why would Dad even agree to that? Was this Rhodes guy so nefarious that he felt it necessary?

Nora continued to read, realizing that the document had been drawn up by her own father! Not Scott Rhodes. If the contract was breached by Scott, all agreed monies would be cut off and Rhodes's transgressions would be made public.

What transgressions? Nora? Had to be.

Nora snagged her phone and searched for Scott M. Rhodes.

Gaping at the image before her, a fresh wave of tears fell. She'd always wished for her father's eyes. Looked like she got her wish after all. She may have Mom's hair and lips, but her face shape, eyes and nose belonged to Mississippi senator Scott Rhodes.

Married for almost forty years. Three children. All a bit older than Nora.

Mom had said she was twenty-two when she'd had Nora, but according to the dates on the documents, Mom had been eighteen when she'd had Nora. Which meant she'd been lying about her age. Claiming to be older than she was. Was this one of his secrets too?

Nora continued to read the history on Scott Rhodes until her stomach roiled.

A man dedicated to wholesome values. An article about families eating meals together popped up with him sitting around a dining room table with his wife and children—minus Nora, who had been a mistake. Someone to throw away and forget about.

Who did this man think he was? That he could sail through life with Dad's money as if Nora never existed. Like red-hot bubbles, anger boiled over until Nora saw nothing but rage. Before she knew it, she was grabbing her coat, slipping on her boots and racing out the front door.

She couldn't handle any more. The walls were closing in on her. She couldn't breathe.

No one would give her answers. She'd take them.

This man who shared her eyes would look into hers and admit he'd abandoned her. Not even that—but had never even cared.

She drove all the way to airport, white-knuckling the steering wheel as she slipped and slid across the icy roads, hoping flights wouldn't be too delayed or canceled. Tourists were still making it into town. Surely she could make it out. When she got to the parking garage, she called a journalist friend with the news station she'd worked for to get an address for the great senator who focused on family values.

Nora needed answers. Clearly, she wouldn't get them from Dad.

But she would get them from her father. She bought the ticket, paced for the entire thirty-minute delay, then boarded the plane to Jackson, Mississippi. She managed to arrive around eleven fifteen. Her friend had texted her the address with no questions asked. She also had several missed calls, voice mails and texts from Rush. She ignored every single one. This was something she would do alone. Nora didn't need Rush standing by and trying to comfort her. She'd lose all resolve. Turn to mush. Maybe even fall apart.

She hailed a cab, climbed inside and rattled off the address. This man would have answers about her mother and if she woke him from sleep, so be it.

As the cab neared Senator Rhodes's antebellum home, some of the fury dissipated and fear burrowed into its place. This man could have had something to do with Mom being in the lake. She had a camera case full of money. He might have asked for more. Was that where Mom was heading? To take him money?

What if he was the one trying to kill Nora now? That

wasn't possible. Mom's death would have made Tennessee news, but not national and doubtfully Mississippi. And he hadn't had time to get to Splendor Pines to spray paint her cabin, but it was possible he knew someone there who had seen the news and called him. But who? That seemed far-fetched.

The cab pulled to the curb and she told the driver to wait. Hopefully this wouldn't take long. She didn't have a ton of cash to spare. She'd maxed out her last credit card paying for the airfare. She stood at the black iron gates locking her out of stomping to the front porch and banging on the door. Gates would not keep her out.

She pressed a button on the intercom and waited silently.

A rattle filtered through the speaker. "May I help you?"

"Scott Rhodes?"

"Who's asking? It's nearly midnight."

"Your daughter. Nora Livingstone." That ought to jerk a knot in him.

The line went silent, but in a few moments, a figure appeared rushing toward her. As the man approached, the sight nearly knocked her breath away. Seemed it did the same to him. He stood staring through the bars, blue-green eyes mirroring hers.

"What are you doing here?" he hissed.

No happy reunion.

"My mom died."

"What do you want me to do about that?" he asked, eyes narrowed. There was no love here either. Not even an ounce. "Do you want money or something?"

Money. Oh, she had debt up to her eyeballs, but she wanted nothing from this man. Besides, her own dad had enough to pull Nora out of debt if she'd ask for it. "I don't want anything but answers. I found the agreement you made with my dad. It was in a safe I stumbled upon earlier this evening."

Scott glanced behind him. "My wife is in the house, upstairs asleep."

"I'm not asking you to wake her up and bring her to the party." Nora wanted to rip his head off. Instead, she forged ahead. "When was the last time you saw my mother?"

"Before you were born. She told me she was pregnant and I told her to get rid it of it." A hard edge formed around his lips.

"*It* is me." How could he stand here and talk about her like she was a thing and not a person?

"You, then. I told her to get rid of you. She said she would."

The man was a liar, but she couldn't tell if he was lying now. "Why did my dad draw up those papers? And did you ever meet him?"

Scott hugged his robe tighter around him. "He came to visit me right after you were born. Said he wanted to raise you as his own. I was concerned he might try to extort money from me—"

"Blackmail you for producing a child through an illicit affair with an eighteen-year-old girl who probably thought you loved her?" Nora nearly spit on the ground. "He is much classier than that."

Cocking his head, Scott studied her, then laughed. "You think she loved me? That I let on like I loved her?" He sobered and his eyes widened. "You don't know, do you?" He laughed again. "Oh, this is rich."

Dread pooled in her gut.

"Your mother was nothing but a high-end call girl. You were an oversight in a business deal gone bad."

Nora couldn't find a single word.

"She didn't want to keep you because she had any imaginings of me leaving my wife. But I didn't trust her not to try to blackmail me or ruin my career. When Joshua Livingstone agreed to pay *me* to have you, I knew he'd keep the secret and not come after me. So I took the deal. It wasn't my first choice, but it's worked so far." His smug smile sent her over the edge.

His first choice would have been to abort her!

"Well, the money stops right now. You won't be getting another penny and if you so much as contact my father, I'll come forward and tell the whole world. And they'll believe it. Because even without DNA testing, I look like you."

That changed his arrogant face. For the first time, he looked afraid of her. Not of getting caught but of Nora.

"And if I find out you had anything to do with my mom's death, I promise you, you'll go to prison. But not before the world and your family know what a piece of slime you are." She balled her fists to keep from shaking in front of him.

Scott hesitated, then spoke. "How do I know you won't come after my money? My career?"

"Because my father raised me better than that." Her father had paid quite a high price to have Nora as his own and was willing to pay until the man before her died.

Another taxi pulled behind hers, lights shining in the distance.

"What is going on?" Scott demanded.

Nora wasn't sure.

Until Rush stepped out of the backseat with fire in his eyes.

Rush stalked to the gate; anger boiled to his brain, but relief that Nora was alive and okay for the moment kept his head level. He'd finally left the pileup on Route 5 only to return to Joshua's and discover Nora wasn't there.

What they'd found on her bed told the tale. Joshua had revealed that he wasn't her biological father. The man who was looked livid and slightly nervous.

Rush approached. Pulled his badge. "Chief Deputy Rush Buchanan. I'm from Splendor Pines."

"Why are law enforcement involved in this?" Senator Rhodes demanded and glared at Nora. "You said you wouldn't tell anyone. Didn't want anything."

"I don't!" Nora's voice rose. "How did you get here?" she asked Rush. "I got the last direct flight and there were delays."

"That's not really what we need to discuss at the moment, now, is it?" He held his temper in check. "I have a few questions about Marilyn Livingstone."

"I already answered those."

Rush listened as the senator recounted his relationship with Marilyn—who he claimed to be a call girl. Joshua hadn't shared that. He might not know. "I'm done talking without my lawyer."

He gave Nora one last glance, turned his back on her—for the second time—and marched toward his home. Rush couldn't imagine the pain and torment she was feeling at this moment.

She'd opted into flying the coop. Hadn't called him, approached her father or stayed put. Nora had possibly put herself in further danger, though Rush didn't have a gut feeling the senator was behind the attacks on her. He wasn't sure if he'd had a hand in anything that might prove nefarious from the night Marilyn died. She did have a case of money.

Now that Nora had revealed everything, Rush couldn't

be certain the senator wouldn't retaliate somehow. But the most important thing at the moment was Nora.

She stood gazing through the bars as if they would open up to her and a new story would unfold. Rush laid a hand on her shoulder. "Nora, it's time to go home."

She rapidly blinked, then inhaled. "Right. Okay."

Rush paid her cabdriver, then guided her into his cab. She gnawed on her nail and stared out the window. Lost in thought. There had to be thousands. "Do you want to talk about it?"

"No. You heard it yourself. There's nothing to say."

There was tons to say! She had to be dying inside, and more than anything, Rush wanted her to lean into him. To talk about her feelings. To know she could confide in and trust him. It was this barrier that had torn them apart and kept them apart. Rush had thought Nora might not be a runner anymore since she'd stuck around to look into her mother's past. But this heavy news had sent her heading for the hills. Physically and emotionally. Proving there were no more shots between them.

"Your dad knows you found the papers. You left them on the bed."

Nora nodded.

"Nora, I know this is a major bomb, but what really matters is that your dad loves you. And he's a good dad. Now you know what he's been hiding." Rush touched her hand, but she pulled away, then slowly she gave it back to him. The simple gesture warmed his heart. He laced his fingers with hers. "Please talk to me."

"If my dad was keeping quiet to protect me from the senator, then he must believe that the senator is dangerous."

Rush didn't mean to talk about the case but if that's all he was going to get, then so be it. "But he couldn't be behind the attacks. That first one at the chalet happened only hours after you arrived in town. Unless he has a connection to Splendor Pines and someone called him and he put out an order. Even then… I'm not sure it's Scott Rhodes."

"Me either. He was genuinely surprised to see me on his doorstep. Mom may have been going to take him money that night and something happened. Either done by him or someone else, but if it was him, why not take the money?"

The cab dropped them at a private hanger. Rush paid the fare and he and Nora crawled out of the cab. "This is how I got to you." He smirked. "When there were no more direct flights, I hit up Buddy Wilkerson."

"Ah Buddy. I didn't realize he was still flying planes."

"On occasion. And he's always been a bit adventurous, so the storm didn't affect him as much as a few extra dollars and doing me a favor did." Rush waved to him and they made small talk before boarding. Once they were buckled in and taxiing, Rush continued, "I agree with you. I don't think the senator is our present-day killer. I can't say for sure if he's involved in the past. But my cousin Hollister was in the navy with a woman who is now a private detective. Lives in DC."

"How would you remember that?" Nora asked.

"He brought her home a few times after you moved to Knoxville. They seemed pretty serious, but it ended. On amicable terms. She can probably look into the senator discreetly. See if we can find any airline tickets or hotels nearby on that night. It's a long shot, but it's all we have."

"Is she how you got Scott's address?"

"Yep."

"What's her name?"

"Theodora VanHolt. She goes by Teddy, though." Rush

leaned back as they ascended. When the plane steadied, he sighed. She may not like what he had to say, but she was going to hear it now that she couldn't make a break for it. Unless she had a parachute. "Nora, you shouldn't have taken off like that. You could have gotten yourself killed. We were all hysterical. Do you not care about the people who care for you?"

Nora squeezed her eyes shut. "You weren't there when I read those papers. You have no idea how it made me feel—"

"And you won't tell me. Ever since your mom died, you've closed yourself off emotionally and physically. You didn't used to be this way. You used to trust me with your hopes, fears and dreams. You can't pin this one on Ainsley. It happened long before her."

Nora started to speak but closed her mouth. Finally, she spoke. "I can't explain what happened to me after Mom disappeared. Or I didn't want to because it would make me a horrible person. The last person I wanted to see me in a bad light was you."

Rush's chest ached to hold her. He cradled her cheeks. "Nora, I could never see you in a bad light. Not then. Not now." Though he was disappointed in her and her actions, there was no hiding the generous, kind and clever woman before him. More than anything he wanted to lean in and kiss her, but now wasn't the time or the place.

"I'm tired. Mentally. Emotionally. Physically."

Rush scooted closer and offered his shoulder. "Rest. We can talk later."

The turbulence didn't seem to affect her. Nora slept right through it all until they landed at Splendor Pines Airport. "How you feeling?" Rush asked.

"I don't know. It's been a lot to take in. Instead of answers I keep getting more questions."

Rush thanked Buddy and led Nora to his truck. They climbed inside. Rush shivered and found his gloves. "I'm going to take you back to the chalet."

Nora nodded and they inched their way toward the cabins. The heat kicked in and warmed the cab of the truck. When they arrived, Rush parked in the driveway of his cabin. "We'll walk over."

Nora only nodded. Her face was pale and her eyes tired, dark circles underneath. Snow crunched under their feet, and Nora leaned into Rush and he put his arm around her.

Crack!

Gunshot. Snow sprayed about a foot from them. "Run!" Rush hunched over Nora, shielding her, and ran behind a tree.

Another shot fired.

And another. Bark splintered. Which was safer—heading for her chalet or into the woods?

Woods. "Let's haul it through there and to your dad's." Someone had been lying in wait. Rush didn't have his radio on him to call it in. But he did have a gun. He fired back, hoping whoever was shooting might change his mind knowing they were armed.

The shooter returned fire.

Grabbing Nora's hand, he hauled her into the woods with him.

When they'd made it deep inside and almost to the stable, the firing stopped. Either they were tracking quietly or they'd given up.

Rush fired one more round to test and see. Nothing.

"Now what?" Nora breathed, air pluming from her lips.

The shooter probably expected them to make a dash to the main house, where he might be tracking to now.

"Let's double back to the chalet and I'll call for backup. Make sure no one gets hurt here or at your dad's place."

Scott Rhodes could have called someone. But the better assessment was someone else had planned this attack. Maybe Ward McKay. Maybe anyone. Marilyn had a slew of deadly secrets, and one of them was out to get Nora.

EIGHT

The morning was overcast and full of snow and ice. Nora hadn't slept a wink. The weight of her mother's past had borne down on her heavily along with the adrenaline from the attack and confronting Scott Rhodes. She picked up her cell phone from the side table: 7:00 a.m. Now she was feeling the exhaustion, but there was no time to sleep. The smell of toast drew her attention to her stomach and it rumbled. Toast. Power must be back on. She plugged in her cell and the lightning bolt lit up.

After brushing her teeth and hair, she entered the kitchen. Dad sat at the table drinking coffee. Tired eyes met hers and for the first time in all her life she glimpsed a measure of uncertainty in them. Nora's stomach knotted.

Conversation time.

Rush cleared his throat. "Pot of coffee and toast. I'm going to go next door and shower. Call me when…" He nodded and grabbed his coat, then bolted.

Nora forced herself to pour a cup of coffee and take a piece of buttered toast from the plate by the coffeepot. "I'm not sure how to start," she said. Tears burned the backs of her eyes.

"Let me start, then." Dad stood. "I love you, Nora.

I love you because you belong to me. I chose you to be mine. I haven't regretted it a day."

Nora's throat tightened and she gripped the counter as she felt Dad's presence move closer to her until she could hear him breathing behind her.

"I love you, Nora."

With trembling lips, Nora turned and faced her father. His deep, dark eyes gazed into hers and tears glossed them over. She fell into his arms and sobbed. "Were you ever going to tell me the truth?"

"No. Because the truth is you're my daughter. Nothing else matters and I wanted to spare you the pain you must have endured last night. I wish you hadn't gone to Jackson."

But she had and she was glad she did. She would have always wondered. Now she knew what kind of monster had created her, the way in which she'd been born. "He said some ugly things, Dad. I don't want to believe them, but I can't ignore them."

"Your mother came here looking for a job."

"At eighteen. I know she lied about her age all these years." Nora sat at the table, unable to stand. This was too much information. Too heavy. Too devastating.

Dad slowly nodded and sat across from her. "She was lost and looking for a place to belong and have you. Something about her moved me. I was way too old for her, and at first it was me giving her sanctuary and a job as a maid."

Her mother. A call girl and a maid.

"But I fell in love with her and I wanted to marry her. I believe she fell in love with me, but her past was tragic." He choked on his own voice. "She was born into an abusive family and she was hurt in every way you could imagine, Nora. When she sought help at sixteen, that man took advantage of her so she ran away."

Nora's heart broke and she sobbed. Mom had been hurt so much, so often. No way to trust anyone. She must have seen the goodness in Dad. His compassion, kindness and generosity. It must have drawn her.

"She lived on the streets awhile in Virginia, where she was from."

"After the house fire that took her family and all the photos?"

Dad sighed. "Those were stories. Your mom didn't want to tell you about her horrific childhood or family. She escaped them."

"They never came looking for her?"

He placed a gentle hand on hers. "They weren't the kind that cared if she left or stayed, I'm sorry to say. She ended up in Jackson, where she met a girl who talked her into making a lot of money. Told her it was safe. Classy." Disgust hung on his words. "That's how she met Scott Rhodes."

Nora covered her face with hands, her mind reeling. "But, Dad, why the affairs? I mean, if she loved you. You were kind to her. You respected her."

Dad's lip trembled. "Sometimes, familiarity is comforting when you don't feel worthy of good things. Of love. Even if familiarity is like going into bondage."

Nora was reminded of the Israelites. Wishing for slavery because they at least got three squares a day and the wilderness seemed uncertain even though God promised to be with them. He'd given them freedom.

"I kept praying and hoping she'd see that I loved her unconditionally and she would change." He rubbed his face, exhausted. "I didn't turn a blind eye. I talked. I ranted. I begged and pleaded with God to let me walk away, to give up, but He seemed to always bring me back to the book of Hosea. Do you know how many times I read it? More times than I can count. Those pages are riddled with tears."

Nora could hardly imagine her dad wetting the pages of his bible in tears.

"But I stuck it out. I reminded myself of her past. The pain. The torment. I did everything I could to prove that she could trust me and was safe."

The bank account. Her own money.

"She struggled her whole life, Nora. But one thing she knew was that I loved her. That she could always come back. Because no matter how exhausted I became, how numb at times and furious at others...down to the bitter end, I loved her."

Nora's heart lurched into her throat. Dad had stayed the course. Kept loving. What if Nora had done the same with Rush? When things got tough. Far less severe than what Dad had experienced. "You knew all this time she was leaving us?"

"Nora, what do you think was happening when she left so many times before? Have you blocked that out?" He clasped her hand. "I told you she was gone on a trip, but, honey, she was leaving. She bolted when things got difficult, when she felt guilt over the affairs. It was hard for her to face me at times. But she always came home because deep in her heart, I know she loved me. And I have no doubt she loved you and Hailey."

Nora could hardly breathe. Mom had left on occasion. Sometimes a weekend. Sometimes a week. Maybe Nora had blocked out the truth to cope. "And Hailey? Is she yours?"

"You're both mine. It doesn't matter."

Hailey might be some other man's child too. But she

couldn't be mad anymore. Not knowing the unimaginable terror and abuse her mother suffered from childhood.

She stood and came around the table and fell on Dad's neck. "I love you, Dad. You are my hero. And I'm sorry for being angry with you over the years. For not fighting to discover the truth." She looked him in the eye. "Do you think Scott Rhodes had anything to do with Mom's accident, that money that was in her trunk or the attacks on me? Is that why you kept so quiet?"

Dad touched her cheek. "Scott Rhodes threatened your mother. If she didn't get rid of you, he would get rid of her. She wanted you desperately so she ran and she feared he'd find her, find you and kill you both."

Nora couldn't fathom it.

"I don't know how much was truth or paranoia, so to put her and myself at ease, I met with Scott. I made the deal and I've honored it and so has he. I don't think he'd rock any boats now due to his upstanding career and the fact that the money was coming in. I have no idea why he might want more money from her. It makes no sense."

"He's not getting any more money. I made it clear. Dad, you're done paying him. But I'm grateful for the lengths you were willing to go to keep me safe. To keep Mom safe and give her a measure of peace."

Dad hugged her. "I'd do it again."

"What do you think will happen now? Do you think he'll come after me?" Two possible killers coming for her? The thought weakened her knees.

"I think he's going to live in a huge amount of fear and paranoia. I think he tried to scare your mother into doing his will. I don't think he'd have ever actually gone through with it. At the end of the day, he's a coward, a liar and a hypocrite." Dad kissed her forehead. "We're all going to be okay."

She wanted to believe that. Wanted to come clean and tell him she'd racked up debt and needed help. After all he'd done for her she couldn't end this conversation with disappointing him. Her mother never had a voice. Never saw justice on earth. She died a victim. Something or someone had her running. "Did you two have any discussions or fights prior to that night that might make her take off?"

"No. Things seemed to be right with us and I'd like to remember that." Dad smiled. He didn't know about the male mask and cuff link in the car. Nora couldn't tell him. He needed the happy memories. She'd give him that. Besides, the mask and cuff link didn't prove she'd had another affair. Only that someone had been in there. Maybe Ward tried to woo her back and that had sent her into making a break for it out of guilt.

"I'd like you to remember that too. Should we tell Hailey? Last we talked she didn't want to know." Nora was sick of keeping secrets—though she was still keeping hidden what had truly brought her home. "I can tell her or we can tell her together."

They decided to tell her together. Not about the possibility that she might not be Dad's biological child either, but all the rest. Rush called and said he'd be over in five minutes. Dad left and Nora's cell phone rang. She answered to the Tampa Bay news station and a job offer at the first of the year, which she accepted. A sliver of regret niggled its way into her chest. Even through the pain and the threats, Splendor Pines was once again feeling like home. But this job was necessary. Dad had forked out enough money on her behalf. She would pay her own debts.

After a few more pleasantries, she hung up and Rush knocked on the door. He wasn't dressed in his uniform but a red-and-gray sweater and dark denim jeans. "How did it go?"

"Better than expected. He doesn't believe Scott Rhodes is behind these attacks or what might have happened with Mom, but he can't be sure. None of us can. Did you get in touch with your private eye friend?"

"I did. She's going to check into it." He searched her face. "Anything else?"

Rush had been pushing her to open up, but she didn't even know where to start, and if she let all her emotions surface, the feelings for Rush would come flooding out too and she was leaving soon. "No. That's it."

The disappointment was visible. It hurt her to see it, but in the end she was sparing them all heartbreak.

"What's your plan today? Staying in your pajamas all day?"

Nora looked down at her reindeer fleece pants. "Wouldn't that be nice. I'm supposed to help Hailey with masquerade inventory. Never was my favorite. You on call?"

"Always. Thought I'd ride out to Mac's and talk to the owner and manager about who Marilyn might have been meeting with."

"I'd like to go with you if you can wait until I'm finished helping Hailey. I can't bail on her."

"No problem. I'll drive you up to the lodge."

Nora paused at her bedroom door. "There is one thing that might be relevant to the investigation. My dad said that during the time leading up to Mom's disappearance they were happy, which is why he wasn't sure why she'd want to run off. She usually did that when things got... difficult." Exactly what Rush said to her last night. She was more like her mother than she wanted to be.

"They were?" Rush asked with a hint of skepticism.

"Yeah. So, let's not tell him about the mask and cuff link. We can't be sure it was there from a man she had an affair with—could be from a man who had a former affair like Ward McKay."

Rush stayed silent.

"I mean, you're the king of not speculating or ruining reputations and lives. Has that changed?"

"No. Nothing's changed."

Except for the fact that she was leaving right after the New Year.

Rush stewed while helping Hailey and Nora unpack boxes. He was good for heavy lifting, but not leaning on for emotional support.

With each hour, the day grew darker, colder. Yet shuttles arrived one after the other with excited tourists chattering about the masquerade ball coming up and how wonderful a snowy Christmas would be. Icy more like it. Like the way Nora reacted to his prompts to open up to him. He couldn't deny feelings surfacing; they were like unwanted weeds in a garden. Rush would pull them but couldn't get to the root. He wasn't looking for a one-sided relationship.

"You ready?" Nora asked, and brushed her hands on her jeans.

"Yep. Might take a while with the road conditions." Rush led her to the Bronco.

"I haven't even thought about a dress and mask," Nora said as she buckled up. "You coming?"

"I'm sure I will. You're gonna be there, right?" Pulling onto the main road, he slowed. The snow had been dozed away but it was still slick. Barely any traffic. Good.

Nora chewed on her bottom lip.

"What's eating at you? And don't say it has anything to do with something to wear to the masquerade."

Nora wrung her hands. "I was offered the job in Tampa. I have to be there after the New Year."

Rush's heart sank. "I see. Well…good for you, Nora. I hope you enjoy the sand and sun. I'm sure you'll be great." He could feel her eyes on him, but he refused to look at her. He shouldn't be this upset about her leaving. "I imagine your family will miss you, especially since they've had you home longer than usual." More like he was becoming used to having her here. Knoxville wasn't too far away, but it wasn't like he could see her every day.

"Yeah. I'll miss them too."

Why did she need a change? What happened in Knoxville?

"Hey, I was thinking. Harvey Langston's wife moved with their daughter too. Remember how upset Dan was over that?" Nora asked.

If Tina Langston hadn't moved, Dan might be married to her and not Ainsley. He'd been crushed. Sheriff Parsons had been pretty worried about him, and let Rush spend a lot of school nights over at their house. "Yeah, I remember." Tina hadn't wanted to move away. "We can talk to Dan. But he's stayed close with Harvey over the years. I doubt he believes Harvey would have had anything to do with hurting Marilyn. And again—"

"We don't know she was hurt by foul play. We don't know she wasn't either. Look, maybe it was all an accident. I still want to know what happened that night. Who was in the car with her and why did she have all that cash? Where does Scott Rhodes fit—if at all?"

"I don't know, but Dan's office is on the next block. He works for Ainsley's dad." Rush pulled up next to Dan's Ford truck and went inside.

Lenora—the receptionist—gave a welcoming smile. "Hey, Rush. What can I do for you?"

"Dan in his office?" he asked.

"He is. Go on back."

Rush led Nora to the offices and knocked on Dan's door.

"Come in."

Rush entered, Nora behind him.

Dan stood when he saw Nora. "I heard you were back in town." He came around the desk and hugged her. "How ya doin', Nora? Heard you left the news station in Knoxville. Where you planning to go?"

"Florida. How are you?"

"Fair to middlin'. What can I help you with?" he asked and looked at Rush.

"Information hopefully. We're trying to trace Nora's mom's steps that night she disappeared. And the days before."

Dan frowned. "Dad said it was an accident. You find something new?"

"Nothing I can divulge, you know that. Did Tina ever talk to you about her dad having an affair with Marilyn?"

Dan shifted his gaze to Nora, discomfort twisting his lips.

"It's okay, Dan," she said. "I'm aware of my mother's indiscretions. Whatever you know will be helpful."

He rubbed the back of his neck. "Tina said her parents fought about it. Got real heated and her mom threatened Harvey and your mom, Nora. Just words, though. I seriously doubt Sheila Langston hurt your mom. She said Harvey promised to end it, but it was too late. Sheila filed for divorce and y'all know the rest."

Sheila might not have hurt Marilyn, but what about

Harvey? "Do you remember seeing Harvey the night of the masquerade ball?"

"Yeah. Can't say what time or anything, but he was there."

"What did he have on? You remember?" Rush asked.

Dan laughed. "How can I forget? He tripped over his stupid cape on the stairs, spilled his drink and cussed. I don't think I'd ever heard him cuss before. Pretty funny."

A cape? Rush's gut twisted. "Mask?"

"White. Covered half his face." He shrugged. The Phantom of the Opera.

Harvey could be the man Rush saw kissing Marilyn that night. And now that Nora clung to the hope that Joshua and Marilyn were in happy at that time, Rush couldn't tell Nora the truth and ruin her last image.

"How long you in town for?" Dan asked Nora.

"First of the month."

"Well, don't be a stranger."

They left the office and climbed back inside the Bronco. Rush pulled onto the street. "Harvey could have been the man in the car."

"I know. He may have promised his wife it was over, but when she left him anyway it made him angry. Harvey may have at the least been in the car to have a heated conversation. At the most, he had something to do with the accident. I wish the striations weren't inconclusive! At least we would be piecing the night together to follow the money in the trunk, not possible murder."

If Harvey was the Phantom of the Opera, his mask and cuff link weren't in the car over a heated conversation. Keeping the secret needled him, but he remained silent.

Ten minutes later, they pulled into Mac's Bar and Grill parking lot, which was mostly empty. Inside there were only a few patrons at the bar. Three couples in booths.

The air smelled of grease and smoke. Rush's stomach rumbled. He hadn't eaten since the toast. "You want to order. If we buy something the owner might be more apt to talk with us."

They sat in a red leather booth near the bar. A young girl with a swinging blond ponytail approached. "What can I get ya?"

"Is the owner in?"

"Mac? No. He's in the Bahamas for Christmas. Wish I was."

"Me too," Nora said.

She'd get warmer weather soon enough. They placed their orders—burgers and fries. "What about the manager?" Rush asked.

"Joe?" She laughed. "He's been around since the dinosaurs. He's in the back. You need him?"

"We do," Rush said, and she disappeared. "I hope she means he's been here for a long time and not that he's old."

Nora chuckled. "Same. After this, we should go see Harvey. I'd rather talk to him in person than over the phone. I want to see his face. Faces are so much more telling than voices."

"I agree."

An older man with a large bald spot and frail arms approached. "I'm Joe Rooney. Can I help you?"

Rush shook his hand. "I hope so. Did you by any chance work here seventeen years ago?"

"I've been here for almost thirty years."

Rush glanced at Nora. "Do you remember a woman named Marilyn Livingstone?"

His eyes softened and he shook his head. "Rotten shame to hear she's been gone all these years, dead in the lake. She was a lot of fun."

"What kind of fun?" Rush asked, hoping it wasn't the illegal kind.

"Lot of laughs. She always had a new joke. Cheesy but funny."

Nora remained silent, but Rush recalled all the jokes she'd tell him that her mother had told her. She had a big joke book Nora had bought her one year as a Christmas gift. He'd helped her pick it out. "Did she come in here often, and do you know who with?" Rush showed him his deputy badge.

"Yeah. About once or twice a week." He sniffed and pointed to the booth in the corner. "Sometimes alone. Sometimes with a friend."

"Any particular friend?" Rush asked.

Joe shifted from one foot to the other. "I don't like ratting out people, but I liked Marilyn and if something bad happened to her I want to help. Langston. Harvey Langston came in with her often, but he's not the only one."

"Who else?" Nora asked.

"I don't know…"

"It would be helping Marilyn, I promise," Rush said. "You can trust me to be discreet."

"Can I trust you to keep my name out of it?" Joe asked.

"I'll do my best."

Joe licked his lips and leaned down. "Right before she went missing she came in several times with…Troy Parsons. Your boss—the sheriff."

NINE

"Rush, my mom was seeing Troy! What are we going to do about that?" Nora buckled her seat belt. The hits kept coming.

Rush pawed his face. "I don't know. Let's not jump to conclusions. It could have been anything."

"Then why not admit it then or now?"

"It might not have been pertinent to the case."

"Or it might have. That would give him motive and a front seat to your investigation." Troy would have a lot to lose if he'd been involved with her and he'd have a lot to protect now to make sure it didn't get out. "Rush, I know he's a mentor to you."

"He's more than that, Nora." Rush leaned his head against the steering wheel. "He's been a father to me. Especially in the past several years."

Nora laid a hand on his back, soothing him. "What does that mean? You've been acting strange about your dad since you put off talking to him about the investigation, and he didn't go to church with your mom, which you never gave a real reason for. He isn't pastoring anymore. Talk to me, Rush."

He lifted his head from the wheel and laughed hard and humorlessly. "You can't expect to bottle up every single emotion and hide things from me, then demand I talk to you. That's not fair."

"You're right. You don't have to share anything you don't want to." And neither did she, but she felt the sting and knew it was the same one Rush endured every time Nora refused to talk intimately with him.

Rush started to say something but his phone rang. "I gotta take this. It's my mom." He answered. "Hey, Ma. Everything okay?…Yeah." He grinned. "Okay. Can you give me an hour or so? I need to take Nora home…Uh…" He glanced at Nora, his neck flushed. "Sure." He hung up. "My family have made it in. I'm shocked they even tried. People don't have the sense God gave them."

She could testify to that.

"You don't have anywhere else to be, do you?" he asked.

"We have somewhere to be. The police station talking to Troy and finding out why he was meeting up with my mom outside of town. Don't let this slide, Rush. He could be impeding the investigation if he's guilty. From the weather to—"

"Not everyone can remember weather facts from twenty years ago." Rush's face soured. "And I never said I'd let it slide. But will a few hours kill us?"

"Maybe! Maybe they will." Nora's frustration rose to stroke levels. "Someone wants me dead. Every second is critical. But let's go have some Christmas festivities."

Rush ground his jaw. "I need to think about my approach, Nora. I need the time, and while I'm figuring it out, I'll keep you safe. You have my word." He headed onto the main road.

Nora studied his face. Rush wasn't just upset, he was rattled and broken. She heaved a sigh, her heart reaching out. A small breather might do them some good. She'd needed time to process everything; Rush did too. "I'm sorry. For my actions and that someone you care about might not be who he lets on to be." She understood completely. "Let's go visit your family. Take a beat." And while she was there, she'd talk to Pastor Buchanan herself. If he had to look her in the eye, he might offer up information that he hadn't to Rush.

Rush nodded, his nostrils pulsing and jaw working overtime. As they neared Rush's family's home he slowed the vehicle. "My dad isn't the same man you knew." He bit his lower lip. "After you left for Knoxville, he counseled a congregant with an addiction to pornography, which had developed into soliciting prostitutes. But after a period of time, the man seemed to be healing and doing well. He had his family back."

Nora nodded for him to continue.

"One night Dad got a call about an illegal gambling and prostitution ring out in the woods near the end of the county line at a pool hall. They raided it and guess what? The man—Randy—was inside. He claimed innocence but refused to explain why he was there. Knowing his history, Dad arrested him for gambling and soliciting prostitutes."

Nora feared the rest of story but listened as Rush told of that arrest, which led to losing his family again. The rumors that spread.

"Randy hung himself but left a letter that stated, once again, he was free of the addiction, loved his family and wasn't guilty, but couldn't live with knowing his family and friends didn't believe him. Many heard about this terrible addiction for the first time. It was horrible."

Nora touched Rush's shoulder. "Was it true?"

"No." Rush's voice cracked. "The truth came out. Randy was trying to give back and help others bound by the same addiction. He found out a young man he was mentoring had gone and he went to get him out. The man had only been married two years and had a newborn. Randy didn't want to give him up and hoped that Dad would believe him. But he hadn't. Not because of the evidence. Randy wasn't actually with a prostitute or at the gambling table. But based on what he knew from pastoral counseling. He'd falsely accused a man and it wrecked dozens of lives, including my dad's."

"I'm so sorry, Rush." No wonder he was hypercareful to avoid rumors. Scandal. It had turned his own world upside down.

"The church board asked my dad to resign. If he was going to use what was said in confidence to accuse someone, they didn't think he could be trusted, and then there were remarks that he lacked discernment. It crushed him, along with the guilt."

Rush had been close with his father. It must have been terrible to go through.

Rush pulled into the driveway crowded with vehicles. "He hasn't healed. He's closed off to everyone. Lost all joy. We keep praying…"

Nora laced her hand in Rush's and squeezed, hoping it would bring comfort. "He'll get it back," she said. "I'll believe it with you." She hadn't believed in anything for so long. But she would believe in this with Rush. It was much easier to believe for someone else. "We'll do it together."

He stared at their hands, traced her finger with his index. Was he thinking of the ceramic Christmas ornaments like she was? The pledge behind that gift. To give him her heart. Always. Forever.

Snow had covered the windshield like a curtain, hiding them. Rush didn't bother to switch on the wipers. Instead, he brushed the thumb of his free hand across Nora's jaw, then let her cheek rest against his palm, calloused but strong, like Rush. He wasn't only physically powerful, he had an inner strength that drew her heart to him.

He met her eyes, held them.

She swallowed.

Slowly he met her lips with his. Familiar. Surprisingly new. At first it was soft as a whisper, as if asking permission to be more intimate. She granted it, allowing him freedom to set off a fire of a dozen suns within her, enough to melt away the ice outside. Unable to catch her breath, she didn't care. Even his kisses were powerful, yet tender like the man. He'd always been special, unique. His fingers slid into her hair. She touched his scruffy cheek before wrapping her arms around his neck as he took his time exploring and savoring.

The beating on the driver's-side window abruptly brought the kiss to a halt. Nora jerked back, her fingers pressed to her thoroughly kissed lips. Rush sighed, didn't bother to even turn and see who was pounding on the window.

"We're going to talk about this later," he said, his voice husky and breathless.

He opened the door and nailed his cousin Hollister in the shoulder.

"Oomph!" Hollister said through laughter. He hadn't changed much. Maybe got a bit better looking if that was possible. What was it with the Buchanan genes? "Didn't mean to interrupt." He cast amused eyes on Nora. "Well, well. Nora Livingstone. I see you still got it bad for this loser."

She couldn't really defend herself after that kiss.

His sister peeped out from behind him. "I told him not to come out here messing with the two of you, but he doesn't listen." She came around to her side and Nora opened the door and hugged Greer Montgomery.

"How have you been?" Nora asked.

"Busy. Moved back to Alabama. And I'm a mom now."

No mention of a husband. Nora didn't pry. "Congratulations."

"Baby girl."

"Can't wait to see her."

"Come inside and you can. We'll leave these men to act like the apes they are."

Nora snickered and followed Greer. Maybe Rush would forget that kiss and they wouldn't have to discuss it. Doubtful. That wasn't the kind of kiss one forgot.

Inside, she was welcomed by everyone, the house crowded with family laughing, joking and eating an array of desserts.

In the corner of the living room, Pastor Buchanan sat alone. Time hadn't been kind to the aging process. She made her way over. "It's nice to see you again."

He patted her hand but didn't make much eye contact. "How you been, Nora?"

"Better."

"Me too. Me too." She couldn't bring herself to bombard him with questions and press him for answers that he might not even have.

Nora caught Rush's eye. His expression was tender and emblazoned with an emotion she didn't want to put a name to. Couldn't. She was too afraid.

Rush stood in the bathroom staring in the mirror and still feeling that kiss. For a moment, it was just a man and a woman in that car. No law enforcer. No weather professional.

No past holding them apart.

No pain.

No fear of the future.

And he'd lost himself. In her eyes that had held longing. In her hands that had intertwined with his to bring comfort, companionship and hope. A woman who seemed hopeless herself was going to believe with him for healing for his dad. That kiss had been his wordless way of revealing how much that meant to him.

How much she meant.

But she was moving, and he'd be left once again watching with a broken heart.

Leaving the bathroom, he entered the festivities and after a few hours of eating and playing games—Nora right in the middle as if she'd always belonged—his phone rang.

Troy.

Stomach in knots, he answered and returned to the bathroom for some privacy. "Hey. What's going on?"

"Got the ballistics from a bullet in the tree the night you were shot at. They're from your gun."

The stolen gun from Nora's. Ballistics were easy enough to follow up on. No reason not to trust the report.

"Have you found any new information?" Troy asked.

Now would be a good time to ask him about his involvement with Marilyn. But Rush wanted to look him in the eye, see his face. "Not much. I'll let Nora know."

"Where are y'all?"

"My folks' place. Probably be here an hour or so longer. But I'm available if you need anything."

"I'll let you know. Bring me a slice of pecan pie." He chuckled and hung up.

"Rush," Nora said as the knock came.

He opened the door. "You need in?"

"No, just looking for you. I thought I heard you in here talking to someone."

"Troy. The gun used to shoot at us was the same one stolen from the chalet."

"What did he say about meeting my mom?" Her eyes drilled into his.

Rush's neck heated. "I didn't ask. I want to do it in person."

Nora's eyes narrowed and she poked a finger in his chest. "Rush, you need to talk to Troy. You've had time to process—at least all the time you can. If he's involved, he's trolling around with a badge and power to destroy evidence and who knows what."

Rush snorted. "You sound like a dramatic crime show. Troy has never once abused his power. I'm sure there's a logical explanation and I'll find out what it is."

Nora gritted her teeth and inhaled. "I've had every imaginable tragic thing thrown at me in a few days' time. When I found out Scott Rhodes was my dad, I went straight there, knowing it wasn't going to be pretty. It's your turn, Rush. Nothing about this has been logical. Nothing."

And what happened when he confronted Troy and found out he was wrong? What would that do to their friendship? Their mentorship? His run for office? No, that wasn't the most important thing, but it was a dream of his. Was he supposed to throw it away because Nora wanted to charge like a bull? "I just need my bearings in order. Figure out how I want this to go down."

"Be a straight shooter—"

His phone buzzed and an alert popped on-screen. He glanced down. "Nora, I gotta go. My alarm at the house is going off." He flew down the hall toward the front door. "Stay here with my family. I'll be back."

Hollister met him at the front door. "What's wrong?"

"Alarm going off at the house." Could be a glitch, a tree falling against a window or the roof, or it could be something else.

"I'm going with you," Nora insisted.

"No, you're not."

She grabbed her coat from the coatrack in the foyer. "Watch me!"

Rush growled. No time to argue. "I have to take the snowmobile." It would take too long in the Bronco.

"And? Let's go!"

"If you need me, call," Hollister said.

Rush ran out the door and to the shed, Nora on his tail. He opened the shed doors, grabbed two pair of goggles, tossed one and a helmet to Nora and they climbed on.

He raced across the snow like sailing over smooth glass. Nora tightened her grip around his waist, leaning into his back. The wind bit and sliced at his skin as they raced through the snowy woods and embankments to his cabin. They made it to the winding drive to his house and he slowed the snowmobile down, then stopped.

He removed his helmet, grabbed his gun. He wasn't sure what to do with Nora. Leaving her on the snowmobile gave her a fast way to make tracks if necessary, but if guns were involved, she was a sitting duck.

"Stay close to me," he said. Having her near meant he could protect her.

The front looked clear. The alert on his phone indicated the kitchen window had been breached, which was in the back of the house. Staying below the windows and scanning the surrounding area, he and Nora made their way behind the house. The window had been busted out and the door was open. "Looks like he went in the through the window and came out the door." Whoever *he* was.

"What do you think he was after?" Nora asked.

"The only thing I can think of is the box of photos. He tried to steal them from you so it's not a stretch." Rush toed the back door farther open, entered and cleared the kitchen. "Stay right behind me."

She did as he instructed and followed him through the downstairs as he cleared all the rooms, including the study where he'd kept the photos. They were missing. "Well, that tells us what he was after."

They cleared the upstairs and returned downstairs.

Rush massaged the back of his neck. "I think the intruder knows he can be identified. By the mask or the cuff links or both. Or maybe he's in a picture with your mom that I haven't found. I don't know."

"Now what?"

Good question. "Now I take you back to my family's house, and I'm going to go have a chat with Troy. I am a straight shooter, Nora. I'm just careful."

Nora threw her hands in the air. "I feel like I keep saying I'm sorry, but I am."

Rush tugged at her hair playfully. "I know. I'm going to leave the snowmobile here and take my truck. I don't like us being so open right now."

Nora agreed and they headed for the garage and climbed into Rush's personal truck. He hit the garage door and slowly backed out of the drive. The wind rocked the vehicle like their lives at the moment.

Mountains and forest flanked the road that narrowed around the curve. What little sun that had been peeking through had dipped below the horizon, and the moon was blocked by the heavy cloud covering.

"What if Troy tells you their involvement was romantic?"

"Doesn't make him a killer. Just a colossal disappointment," Rush said, and spied headlights coming around the curve behind him. He couldn't tell if it was a truck or SUV, but it had to be tourists. No local would go this fast and this close to another car on the road.

Rush pressed the gas, but he didn't want to go too fast with the road conditions.

The vehicle kept coming.

"Nora, hang tight. I think we have trouble."

The other vehicle made impact.

Nora yelped.

Rush's truck spun in circles across the icy road.

"Rush!" Nora hollered as they went over the side of the road and down the ravine.

TEN

Rush's truck plummeted over the side of the road, tail end first, banging them into rocks and tree branches. Metal crunched and scraped as he prayed and endured.

Nora knocked her head against the window and went limp.

Rush was helpless.

"God! Save us!"

He hit the emergency brake, hoping it would slow them down before they crashed to their deaths. The truck slowed minimally, and then it rocked and pitched onto the passenger side. Rush's seat belt cut into his skin as the flipping of the vehicle battered his body and knocked the wind from him. Glass shattered.

Tree branches poked through the pulverized windshield. Rush's face stung and burned.

The truck rolled again and again. If it continued down the mountain, they wouldn't make it. "Nora," he choked out. Blood trickled down her forehead. "Nora!"

She wouldn't answer.

It felt like every bone in his body was breaking; his head pounded and his ears rang.

Sudden impact jarred him, and he bit his tongue. Every nerve in his body screamed.

But they'd stopped rolling.

The truck was lodged in a huge pine. Snow dropped onto their bodies through the missing windshield. Rush's hands were cut up. It hurt to move. To breathe. But he didn't know how long the tree would break their fall.

They were a fourth of the way down the mountain if he guessed right.

"Nora," he choked out again and undid his seat belt while thanking God they'd at least landed upright. *God, give me strength.* He was nauseous and dizzy.

His driver's-side door butted up against the side of the mountain, and Nora's door hung open. Nothing but branches and evergreen.

The only way out was through the open windshield, and then they'd have to find a way to climb up the snowy terrain to the road.

It seemed hopeless.

A gale rocked the truck. No time to waste. He needed Nora to wake up this minute.

"Nora." He lightly shook her for fear of serious injury. If she was unable to move… How would he ever get her out and up a steep mountain with no climbing gear?

She stirred and moaned.

"Nora Beth, can you hear me?"

"Rush." She moaned again and shifted.

"Don't move, Nora."

Her eyes fluttered open, glassy at first, then they focused on him and panic shot through them. "Rush!"

"Don't move," he repeated. "We're in the pines and it's not secure. We went over the edge of the mountain. How bad are you hurt?"

"My head hurts and…my everything hurts." She wiggled her fingers. Cuts and scrapes covered her face and neck.

"Anything major?"

"I don't know. I don't think so."

That in itself was nothing short of God's divine protection over them. "We have to get out through the windshield. Go first. Onto the hood, then grab on to those branches for support. We'll use rocks and stumps to anchor us as we climb."

Her eyes grew to the size of dinner plates.

"We have no other choice. We can do it." He hoped his confident words masked how he actually felt.

Rush had lost his phone from the console and Nora's purse was missing. No one to call for help. The Lord would be their very present help. That was a promise in the Scriptures he was going to stand on. In this case... climb on.

The night was bleak and dark. Only the headlights gave a soft glow. This trek would be one done blindly. Fear raced through him.

Nora unbuckled and winced. Groaned.

"Be easy. Go slow but fast," Rush said. "I'll be right behind you."

"I'm scared, Rush. I don't know if I can." Nora's faint voice shook with uncertainty and terror. He was scared too.

"You can do it, Nora. We've climbed mountains together before."

"We've had climbing gear and it wasn't in winter."

"Let's pretend we have them now. And light to guide our way. It'll be a fun challenge. We'll look back on it years from now and laugh."

"Yeah, right." She leaned forward and the truck jerked; the cracking of tree branches tore through his heart. If the branch broke...

Nora paused, breath pluming in front of her.

"Keep going," Rush offered. If nothing else, he could

at least get her out. Keep her safe and alive. He'd worry about himself later. Nora's safety was his focus.

Hopefully her leather gloves would protect her from the small shards of glass littered across the dashboard. With shallow breaths, Nora placed her hands on the dash and lifted herself from her seat, groaning in pain, but she managed to get her head out of the windshield and her hands onto the hood of the truck.

The wind shook snow onto her body and she flinched. His truck shuddered again and she squealed.

Carefully, Rush helped her scoot all the way onto the hood. "Can you see a branch or rock or anything to hold on to?"

"I can't see anything, Rush! I'm gonna die out here!"

"No one is dying, Nora Beth! Find something! Once you have it, let me know and I'll come out next."

Nora turned and looked at him. "What if I can't? What if the truck falls when I climb off it?" Hysteria laced her tone.

"Listen to me," he pleaded. Fear would keep her glued to the truck and they'd both end up at the bottom of the mountain. "Climb on top of the truck and grab a tree branch."

She nodded and slowly stood, placing her hands on the top of the truck. Wind battered her; she nearly lost her balance.

The branch splintered and cracked further; Rush's heart raced. "Go, Nora!"

Nora used her arms to push herself on top of the truck. The sound of metal above him told him she was reaching. "I got a branch… I'm on the mountain. Come out."

Now the tricky part. He had to move onto the console without kicking the gearshift sticking out beside his steering wheel.

He grabbed the lever to push the seat back so he could maneuver. The branch shook and the truck did too. He froze, didn't breathe.

"Rush!" Nora called. "Hurry up!"

Now that he had more legroom, he lifted his right leg and swung it carefully over the console, then using his arms for support lifted himself up and slid onto the console. Once he was in position, he made his way through the open windshield and onto the hood.

Wind howled through the trees and it began to sleet again, but his adrenaline chased away the cold.

About three feet up, Nora clung to a branch.

"I'm coming. Hold on." He didn't want her to get ahead of him. If she slipped, he wanted to be behind her to catch her. Again, using his arms, he lifted himself to the top of the truck, but his foot swung inside the windshield, kicking the steering wheel and turning the tires.

The branch cracked and the truck dropped farther down. Rush lost his balance and slid; his heart pounded.

He grabbed the door, holding on and thankful the window was no longer there. Feeling with his foot, he worked to find a solid hold.

Wood splintered at deafening levels, and his body screamed in pain.

His throat tightened and sweat ran in trickles down his temples.

The truck plummeted and he let go, catching a branch and hanging on by a thread.

"Rush!"

"I'm—I'm here," he called. He found footing and worked his way up, slowly, steadily—slipping every few feet. It was snowy, rocky, uneven ground and slick from ice, but he made it to Nora.

"That scared me half to death," she said through chattering teeth.

"Back at ya. Up ya go. Be slow."

She found another limb and used it for support as they made their way up the mountain. Nora stumbled and Rush caught her with one hand to steady her.

"Who—who do you think hit us?" she asked.

"Someone who knows how to drive on icy roads. Stop talking and concentrate on getting to the top."

Heaving, shaking and fighting for every step forward, they finally reached the top and collapsed on the shoulder of the road. Rush didn't care that he was lying in snow. But a chill would come and they couldn't afford to get sick. Nora lay beside him breathing heavy.

"How you doing, Nora Beth?"

"Well…let's just say 'over the hills we go' is no longer appealing to me."

Rush laughed. "Amen." Time to get out of the elements and dry. "Come on." He pulled her to her feet. "We're hoofing it."

"I'm not sure I can walk very far, Rush."

He wasn't either but they had no plan B. Nora had been brave and resilient. She could make it a few miles more. Gently wrapping his arm around her shoulders, he coaxed her forward. "You can do it. I know you can."

Hunching from the snow and sleet, they trekked about a half a mile when headlights came into view.

Rush's stomach knotted.

Blue lights flashed.

"The cavalry."

Nora bristled against him as the window rolled down. Inside, Troy Parsons eyed them and smiled.

* * *

"Y'all look like you've been rode hard and put away wet. What happened?" Troy asked.

Nora clutched Rush's arm. Mighty convenient Troy being out on the road on this side of town an hour or so after they'd been sent over a mountain. Nora didn't trust him. Not even a little, and she hoped Rush didn't either. Not after what they discovered earlier today.

"Someone sent us over the cliff. 'Bout a half mile back," Rush said with steely eyes. Looked like he had the good sense to suspect Troy. "After we left Mama and Dad's."

Troy sobered, and he shone a flashlight in their faces. "Get in! I thought y'all just broke down. You need a hospital."

Nora didn't want to get in the vehicle with Troy. What if he was lying? Rush glanced at Nora and patted her hand. "All right." He opened the back door of Troy's Bronco. "Get in, Nora Beth." He urged her to get in the backseat, but she wasn't sure that was a smart idea. "We have to," he whispered in her ear.

He was right. The cold was catching up to her. Sweat had turned to chills. The crashing of adrenaline had her shivering on top of the cold. Their hair was soaked with sweat, snow and sleet. Reluctantly, she eased into the backseat. Her body was aching and stiff everywhere.

Rush closed her door and hobbled to the passenger side. He got in the front seat and strapped in.

Troy glanced in his rearview. "I'm taking you to the hospital. Don't even start, Rush."

Nora touched the cut on her head. She wouldn't turn down some heavy meds, but mostly she wanted warmth and a cup of hot tea.

"What exactly happened?"

Rush told him the gist of the story as Troy drove them to the ER. "I can't help but think it came on the heels of us visiting Mac's today." Rush studied Troy. Nora couldn't see Troy's face from the backseat, but she didn't miss the tightened grip on the steering wheel at the mention of Mac's.

"Oh, yeah?" Troy asked. "Find out anything important?"

Yes! Tell him, Rush.

"Mac's in the Bahamas. We didn't get to talk to him."

What? *Rush!* Why was he not questioning Troy? This man might have information, and the fact that he wasn't coming forward with it meant he wanted it to stay a secret. He'd already been adamant it was an accident, lied even—possibly—about the weather conditions that night. Nora had been checking into it, but she hadn't had the proper time to access the many different sites necessary for the research. Not with all the attempts on her life.

Exhaustion was setting in and she didn't have time to be tired. There were too many unanswered questions. Too many puzzle pieces that didn't fit. Pieces Rush should be asking about.

"Shame," Troy said. "Guess you'll have to wait."

Wait? He didn't seem too upset about that.

"Nora, hon, do you think all this investigating has been worth the pain? I'm worried about you," Troy said. "Maybe it's best if you leave this to the professionals and back off."

Someone knocked her down a side of the mountain. Quitting now was never going to happen. "What if it was someone you loved? Would you give up?"

"I'm not asking you to give up. I'm asking you to step down. Difference."

She closed her eyes and trembled. "I can't do that, Sheriff Parsons. I'm not breaking any laws."

He grimaced and moved from her line of sight in the rearview. "You're blessed to be alive right now. I don't want to get a call in the night saying I have to come out to your homicide scene."

She wasn't so sure she believed that, but he was taking them to the hospital. He could have run them over. "Then I suggest you do more than what you've done so far. I didn't see you fighting hard to find my mom seventeen years ago, and I haven't seen you do much of anything now," she spouted as he pulled up to the hospital.

Troy's tone turned hard. "What am I supposed to do about an accident, Nora? The coroner ruled it one. Not me. And I have other things to do besides look into why she left the party, got in her car and had an accident. You may not have closure, Miss Livingstone, but *this* case is closed. I've only let Rush work on it as a favor to you because of y'all's history. But it's put him in danger."

"Troy," Rush warned.

"No, it's true. Your life has repeatedly been in danger—"

"Which proves something sinister is going on!" Nora cried. "Why would someone want me dead if something bad didn't happen that night?"

"Maybe it did, Nora. Maybe someone from that night doesn't want you digging up an affair and ruining a family that may or may not have gotten back on track. And I'm not being passive on the attempts on your life—I'm making sure bullets have tests run and prints are taken. That is an open investigation. What went on seventeen years ago *is not*!"

Nora bounded from the car, the pain in her muscles protesting. But she slammed the door anyway and stalked inside.

Rush followed and they said nothing while doctors attended to their wounds and stitched the cut on Nora's head. Two hours later, Hailey picked them up and brought them back to the chalet. After changing into dry clothing, Nora eased on the couch with her laptop.

"Before our pain meds kick in, what was that?" he asked. "Back in Parsons's car?"

"That was someone being proactive. That was someone taking matters into her own hands because…well never mind or I'll end up having to apologize again later."

"Ah, so you want to call me names and hurl insults at me again." He huffed.

"You had the chance to question him, Rush. You caved. You're too afraid of hurting his feelings. Or maybe you're afraid to find out the truth—that he isn't the man you thought he was. Well, guess what, Rush Buchanan… no one is! I've learned that." She slammed her laptop on the couch and stood, enduring the pain in her joints. "At least I'm doing something to get the truth for my mom."

Rush inhaled sharply and ran his tongue along the inside of his cheek, his nostrils flaring. "First of all, don't for one second think I believe you're doing all this for truth for your mother. She's gone. She doesn't care about the truth. She doesn't need answers. You want answers to prove she wasn't running, but you already know that she was. This is about you. Answers you won't and can't get." He stalked to her and stood toe-to-toe, his gaze drilling into hers.

"But I've risked my life over and over to make sure you stayed alive and safe while on this hopeless quest because it's what you want. Like I *always* have done whatever you wanted. Because I loved you!"

Nora shrank back from the truth giving her another pounding. Rush was right. Again. As always. She tried to intervene, but he was on a tangent and he rightly deserved it.

"I've kept quiet about what I saw that night. I've given in to all your whims," he yelled. "I've watched you walk away twice! Twice, Nora. Twice you've killed me. And here I am doing what you want—for what? You to yell at me, tell me I'm not doing my job?"

She'd killed him twice. Those words. This whole tirade wasn't fully about the investigation but Rush's heartbreak at Nora's hands. Hands she'd promised to hang on a tree to show her love for him year after year. She was a horribly selfish person.

"And for your information, I didn't question Troy because if he is involved, why would I call him out on it when we were at his mercy? I had no weapon. No control of his vehicle—and things might have been different if you hadn't been inside. But you were, Nora. And I was afraid if he is the bad guy, showing him my hand could have put you in danger."

Nora hadn't thought of that. She'd been too focused on nothing but what she wanted. Answers.

"And as steaming mad as I am right now at you, I'd do it all over again. Because, Nora, I *still* love you! I doubt I'll ever not love you."

What? He…loved her? Now? In the present? "Rush," she whimpered.

He thrust a hand up to halt whatever she might be about to say. "Before you go reminding me that I'm a cheater and you're moving to Florida and all the other excuses, let me tell you all the reasons I'm not going to act on it. You're a runner, Nora. When things get difficult, you take off. Figuratively and literally. And I won't be with a woman who can't open up to me. Who will run from me and not *to* me. So, this time, you don't get to leave me. You don't get to hurt me. You don't get to say things aren't going to happen between us, that we're over. *I'm* saying it."

She blinked back tears, every word crushing her with the weight of its truth and Rush's own pain in every syllable. She'd hurt him. Time and again. She hadn't meant to. Didn't want to, but she had.

"We're never going to happen. And I hate it. I hate having to voice that out loud. Because all I've ever wanted is to love you. To make you happy. To be happy with you. But I don't trust you, Nora. You think you can't trust me because of all those years ago when I was dating Ainsley. But I can't. Trust. You. I can't trust you not to leave. How is that for irony for someone who didn't want to be anything like her mother?" He shook his head, raked a hand through his hair and exhaled an exhausted sigh.

Nora couldn't form a word. He was so right it was scary. Talk about tough love.

"I'm tired, Nora Beth. If Troy isn't the bad guy here, then someone thinks we're dead. I'm going next door to have a minute to myself and I'll be back to bunk on your couch in an hour or so."

He slunk to the front door.

"Rush," she called. "I'm sorry."

"It's kinda too late for that, don't ya think?" He closed the door behind him.

Nora stared at the door for several long beats, then she locked it and leaned against it until she slid to the floor, tucking her knees under her chin. Burning tears exploded from behind her eyes and erupted in sobs.

She *was* like her mother. In more ways than she wanted to admit. What was she going to do with that? *God, I don't know what to do.*

Her world had been crumbling around her for years,

and now it was falling faster than she could breathe in and out. Everything was being stripped away and what was laid bare wasn't pretty. She wasn't who she wanted or needed to be.

Nora had lost herself so long ago, she wasn't sure she would be able to find her true self again.

One thing she did know. It was time for a change. Inside out.

ELEVEN

Rush sat on the couch in Nora's chalet with a cup of coffee warming his hands. He'd popped several meds throughout the night, and this morning he had a dull headache and body aches from yesterday's events. His truck was totaled. Tow truck company was hauling it out this morning. Cell phones were gone. He'd have to get a new one today at some point, talk to Troy and deal with the aftermath of last night.

When he'd returned, Nora was in her bedroom. He'd gone to the door to knock and hoped to apologize. He'd been angry and gruff. Not that what he said wasn't true, but he could have said it with more constraint and compassion. But he'd heard her crying and he couldn't bring himself to knock. Not when she'd called his motives into question about his hesitation to address Troy.

Because it was true.

He'd had plenty of time to talk to his mentor before they went over the side of a mountain. But Rush was afraid of what Troy might say—or what he might not say. When he'd brought up going to Mac's he'd hoped for a better response. He'd known Troy a long time. His boss was hiding something—possibly an affair with Marilyn, which would wreck his marriage and relationship with Dan.

The bedroom door opened and Nora entered the kitchen and living room looking bruised and battered. And beautiful. She left her hair down—likely to hide some of the bruises and abrasions. Her eyes were red rimmed. He stood and rubbed his hands on the sides of his jeans. "Hi," he murmured.

"Hi," she said. "Coffee left?"

"Yeah." He motioned toward the pot. The silence was deafening. Awkward. Uncomfortable. "How you feelin' this morning?"

"Sore. You?"

"Same." His neck muscles were tight and not just from the wreck. "I'm sorry, Nora, for the way I came at you last night."

She paused, then put the carafe back in place and slowly stirred cream into her coffee. Her cherry scent wafted his way.

After sipping her coffee, she turned toward him. "I'm sorry too. I hadn't realized what you were doing and I was…I was scared. But it's not an excuse for accusing you of not doing your job. You're the most honest man I know. Full of integrity and compassion. You'd never lie." She sighed over the coffee cup. "And if I'm being honest…I was scared all those years ago when I found out about Ainsley. Yes, I was mad about what it might do to my reputation, but mostly I was afraid. So I used my anger as a reason to go."

"Afraid of what?" He wasn't expecting this. Nora was opening up a measure.

"That if we got back together—at some point down the road—I'd end up hurting you. And even with us not together, I have. I've hurt you terribly, Rush. And I'm sorry. It's not too late to say it."

Rush wasn't sure what to say or even if he could, not with the lump clogging his throat.

"I've hurt myself too," she said. "I don't share the truth about me or how I feel because I hate the truth. I hate a lot of things about myself. For one, I'm a hypocrite." She set the cup down, hand trembling, but then she raised her chin. "I'm up to my eyeballs in debt. I went to Knoxville to escape this place. Escape being Marilyn Livingstone's daughter. I didn't want that. I made this new life, made connections with the elitists and tried to be someone new, but that someone couldn't keep up with those people—I don't have my dad's money."

Rush stepped forward to go to her, to comfort, but she shook her head and he paused.

"I didn't quit my job. I lost it to someone else. But I didn't want anyone to know that either. You're right, Rush. I've been selfish. And you're also right…you and I…we had something once. We did. But too much has happened between us. We can't ever get that back. I'd hurt you. Like I always do. You're right to have stopped it before it started."

Rush's eyes burned and he clenched his teeth to hold back a dam of emotions.

"And one more truth for today." She inhaled and let out a shaky sigh, but she looked him square in the eye. "I love you too. I don't think I'll ever not love you."

She repeated his words from last night, but instead of filling him with joy it only brought a stabbing pain and ache. There was nothing left to say.

Nora returned to her coffee cup and paused, then straightened her shoulders. "Now. Moving on. Last night, you said something. It didn't hit me until this morning."

Rush mentally trekked through their previous conversation. "I don't know what you're talking about."

"You said, 'I've kept quiet about what I saw that night,' and then kept going. As I replayed that conversation it dawned on me... I have no idea what you were talking about."

Rush's stomach landed at his feet. In the heat of the moment, he'd blurted it. So much for trying to spare Joshua and Nora peace about Marilyn at least being faithful in the end.

"Rush? What are you keeping me from me?"

Rubbing his forehead, he turned around, his back to her. "Nora, I was trying to spare you then and I was going to tell you early on in the investigation but you were still in denial...and then your dad thought everything had ended well—"

"Rush!" Nora grabbed his forearm and spun him around. "What do you know?"

"Your mom was kissing a man with a Phantom of the Opera mask that night. In your dad's office."

Nora gaped, then her eyes lit up. "That's why when I got to the basement, you hurried me away. Said you wanted to exchange presents somewhere else. My mom was in the office with a man! Possibly the man in the car. Probably so."

Rush nodded. "How mad are you?"

"Yesterday, I might have gone off the deep end. But I've been a vault of secrets so I can't really be angry. I'm sorry you had to see that. Sorry you carried that with you all this time."

"I didn't want to hurt you."

Nora's eyes turned watery. "I've done all the hurting, Rush."

They remained silent. No words to be said. Only regret and pain.

Nora gave a tight-lipped smile. "I've almost finished my research. While it's not one hundred percent accurate, it is likely the weather didn't contribute to my mother's car accident. Troy was either lying or he remembered poorly. After what we've discovered, my guess is he was lying."

Rush nodded. "I'm going to talk to Harvey Langston today. I can't be sure he'll tell me the truth, but it's worth a shot."

"I'd like to come with you."

"I know." His phone rang. "It's Teddy VanHolt." He answered and put her on speaker. "Hey, Teddy. It's early."

"Not for you. And I'll sleep when I'm dead."

"I suspect you have news."

"I do. My friend Wilder Flynn at Covenant Crisis Management had his computer analyst do some research for me. I can confirm that Scott Rhodes has been receiving payments from Joshua Livingstone. I cannot confirm the purchase of plane tickets on or around the Christmas Eve in question. Nor did I find any paper or digital trail of him making a road trip to Splendor Pines or any town or city within a day's drive. It appears he isn't directly involved now or in the past."

Rush and Nora had a hunch he wasn't. No, Scott Rhodes had the sweet end of the deal. A lot of money every year his entire life to leave Nora and Marilyn alone. Why rock that boat?

Teddy continued, "I have enough to expose him for soliciting prostitutes and using high-end call girls. I'm always up for leaking anonymous info to the press. Say the word."

Rush looked at Nora and she shook her head. He silently agreed with her. If Scott Rhodes wasn't out to hurt Nora, better to leave him alone. Not that he condoned what Scott Rhodes was doing, but that wasn't for him to expose. Besides if the press dug, they might find Nora and who knows what kind of backlash that would have. "No. Sit on it. Anything recent? Trips here? Any way to know if he hired muscle to come deal with Nora?"

"I don't think so, Rush. Seems your problem is local. Anything I can do to help? Happy to take a trip to the mountains."

"The weather is treacherous. You're safer where you are but thank you."

"No prob. How's Hollister?" Teddy asked.

"He's same old, same old. Is that why you really wanna make the trip?"

Teddy laughed. "If I wanted to know what Hollister was up to, I'd know."

That was the truth. "Merry Christmas, Teddy."

"Merry Christmas, Rush."

He hung up. "What do you want to do, Nora? I think we can safely rule out Scott Rhodes."

Nora nodded. "I agree. Let's pursue the leads we have now, see where they take us."

"Let's start with Harvey Langston."

Harvey Langston hadn't coughed up anything other than admitting he had been involved with Nora's mom for a brief time and it had cost him his marriage. Nora couldn't be sure if he was lying or not, but she still had her sights on Ward McKay. He was shady. He had motive and opportunity as well as connections to hire someone if he wasn't actually doing the dirty work.

But what had Nora up in arms at the moment was the phone call from Hailey. Dalton was sick and she couldn't get away with all the preparations for the masquerade ball. Nora didn't mind picking him up; it was nice to be needed and feel useful.

But the elementary school connected with the middle school, and there might be a chance Nora would encounter Ainsley Parsons. She didn't want to bump into her even if bygones were bygones, according to Rush.

"I can't believe the kids have school," Nora said.

Rush chuckled. "As long as they can keep power and water going, the kids are stuck having to attend and pining for snow days."

"I loved snow days. Poor Dalton won't be enjoying anything."

"You want me to come in with you? Help out if he needs carried or something?" Rush asked.

The idea of him swooping in to carry out a sick little boy sent flutters through her middle. Rush would make a wonderful father. "That's sweet but…but I'd rather go alone." She was dreading bumping into Ainsley. Having Rush with her would be even worse.

"I understand. Text if you need me."

"Will do." She went inside and straight to the office. A fresh-faced brunette sat behind the reception desk. "I'm here to pick up Dalton Gladwell."

"Name?"

"Nora Livingstone," a voice said from behind.

Nora swiveled and shrank inside. "Ainsley. Hello." Well, of course she'd see her right off the bat.

"Miss Livingstone," the receptionist said, "I'll need your license for checkout."

She showed her the photo ID and the receptionist called the nurses' station for them to bring Dalton to the office.

"You can wait in here or on the bench in the lobby."

The lobby. "Thank you." She hurried by Ainsley and into the lobby, where she perched on the bench and prayed Ainsley wouldn't approach her again.

Didn't look like the prayers had reached Heaven yet. Ainsley returned, flaming red hair, dark eyes and a file folder in hand. "How've you been?" she asked as she approached.

"Good. You?"

"Good." She blew a tuft of hair from her eyes. "How about we not let this feel awkward. Chalk up the past to young adult drama."

Nora relaxed. Rush had been right. "I'd like that."

"So you know, I never went blabbing like I said I would. I was hurt, but Rush and I…" She shrugged. "I started seeing Dan a few weeks after that. The rest is history."

"You got a great catch."

"I did." She sighed. "I'm sorry about your mom. That can't be easy."

"No, it hasn't been. But thanks. And I'm sorry about your dad's hotel. We stopped by there the other day to talk to Ward and I couldn't believe it." She also couldn't believe she was sitting here chatting with Ainsley Parsons. The insecurity in her past had made her paranoid. What if she hadn't gotten out of Dodge but stuck around?

"Dad's had some hard knocks but he always gets back up."

"Aunt Nora!" Dalton feebly cried. His little face was pale and his lips cherry red and cracked. "I'm sick."

"I heard, buddy. We're gonna get you home and all snuggled up. Sound good?" She rubbed his head, the heat radiating against her palm. "Has he had any Tylenol?" she asked the nurse.

"No, we're not allowed to administer medicines

without a prescription." She smiled apologetically. "His temperature was 101.2 thirty minutes ago. I gave him a Popsicle and a cool rag."

"Thank you," Nora said.

"Where's my mom?"

"She's covered up right now on the big masquerade ball stuff so here I am. That okay?" Poor kid. When Nora had been young and sick, all she wanted was her mother. She'd have to suffice for now.

"Will you be in town for the ball?" Ainsley asked.

"Yeah. First one in a while."

Ainsley patted Dalton's head. "Feel better, little man. You can't be sick at Christmastime. You have too many sweet treats to eat!" With that, she waved and went back inside the office.

"Flu's going around. I'd have him tested," the nurse said. "Feel better, Dalton."

Nora bundled Dalton into his coat and wrapped her scarf around his head. "Come on, buddy. Mr. Rush is waiting outside, and he's in the sheriff's Bronco. Maybe he'll switch the sirens on for you. That would be fun, huh?"

"Yes, ma'am," he said, and trudged along beside her. She helped him into the backseat, buckled him up and grabbed the flannel blanket from the floorboard, covering him with it.

"I don't know what meds are at the house. Can we stop for some?" she asked Rush as she climbed inside the toasty warm Bronco.

"Of course. Hey, Dalton. Sorry you feel bad." Rush switched on the sirens and Nora's insides turned to marshmallow. She hadn't even had to ask. Dalton's glassy eyes lit up.

"Cool!" he said.

They stopped off at the convenience store for medicine and a few other items. "I'll be right back," Nora said.

She hurried inside, but carefully—the parking lot was slick. Christmas music played over the speakers, and the store smelled like pine cleaner and vanilla. The cashier—who seemed bored to death—greeted her.

Nora strode down the aisle and found the Tylenol. If it was the flu, what else might make an six-year-old feel better? She perused the shelves. Hairs rose on the back of her neck. She glanced up. No one was in the aisle with her. But she had the distinct feeling she was being watched.

She went back to hunting items that might make him feel better. She'd filled her small cart with Popsicles that had electrolytes in them, chicken noodle soup, crackers, 7 Up and a pack of Pokémon cards. No one seemed to be lurking, but Nora couldn't shake the feeling that someone was.

After paying for the items, she hurried with her plastic bags to the vehicle.

"Did you see Ward McKay?" Rush asked as she climbed inside.

"No."

"He left a couple of minutes ago."

Could Ward have been spying on her? Hiding from her, then making his exit before she got to the checkout line? "I won't lie. I felt watched in there, but I never actually saw him. Did he see you when he came out?"

"I'm hard to miss in this vehicle, but he didn't pay me any attention. Didn't wave."

"My tummy hurts, Aunt Nora."

Nora hurried and emptied a plastic bag—just in case. She handed it to him. "We're almost home, buddy. Hold tight and you can crawl in bed soon."

"Main house?" Rush asked.

"Yeah. His movies and bedding are there. Thanks for running errands for us." Rush made it a point to go out of his way for others. She admired his giving spirit and it wasn't only at Christmastime. This was Rush all year long.

Nora opened the Tylenol and poured a dose in the cup. "Here, buddy. Go ahead and take this."

She caught Rush smirking.

"What?"

"Nothing," he said.

"Something."

He chuckled. "I was thinking you'll make a great mom, Nora Beth." His voice became hushed, almost reverent. "You still want kids?"

"I do." She'd dreamed of baby names since she was a little girl. Dreamed of having Rush's last name. "Someday."

"Someday feels out of reach, doesn't it?" Rush murmured. Was he reading her mind or was he speaking quietly for himself?

Hope for them was lost.

Hope for Rush finding love again wasn't.

Nora wasn't sure she'd ever find anyone as special as Rush. She might as well be doomed to live alone forever.

Hope had disappointed her time and again.

The Lord is my portion, saith my soul; therefore will I hope in Him.

The verse from *Lamentations* that hung on the wall in her father's office struck her heart. Had her hopes been in Jesus or in the things she'd longed for and wanted? She glanced at Rush. She'd placed her hope in him as a young girl. When Mom vanished, not even Rush could fill the void and ache.

And she hadn't turned to the Lord for her strength, to soothe her sore soul.

She'd run.

"You okay, Nora Beth?" Rush asked as he pulled into the snowy drive of the main house.

Turning her head to wipe a few stray tears that had escaped, she nodded. "Yeah. Let's get this little man inside and to bed."

Poor little Dalton was looking even more feeble. "I got him," Rush said and scooped the boy in his arms. Tears stung her eyes at the sight. Nora grabbed the plastic bags and they entered the house. "Where's his room?"

"Upstairs. Second on the left. I'll be up after I call Hailey."

Rush started up the stairs with Dalton. He was talking to him, but she couldn't hear the words. Dalton giggled. She sighed and called Hailey.

"How is he? I feel so guilty for not picking him up myself, but these invoices won't get entered by themselves and Nathan couldn't leave work... Don't get me started."

Being a single mom wasn't easy. Nora wished there was more she could do. "I could come enter the invoices for you. Leave me a list of codes and I'll get the hang of it."

"Thanks, Nora. But I'm almost done."

"Okay, well he'll probably go to sleep. I gave him Tylenol on the way here and bought some stuff for him. Rush is putting him in bed now. The nurse said it could be the flu and he'll need to be tested for it. If you can't take him to the doctor, I can." It was the least she could do to help her sister out.

"I'll do it. I'll call now and let you know. Thanks for helping me, Nora. I miss having you around—not for favors but because I just miss you. I wish you weren't taking the job in Florida. Hank always needs help at the radio station."

The original job she'd been coming home to interview for before the fiasco with Rush. "I don't want to work in radio, Hailey. But I do miss you and being here, even though it hasn't been easy. It still feels like home." Unfortunately, Nora couldn't bear to live so close to Rush knowing they could never be together. That felt like punishment.

"I understand. Dalton will be thrilled to come visit you and get beach time in. There are definitely perks." She snickered. "I could use some soaking in the sun on the beach, reading a good book. I can't tell you the last time I had the chance to enjoy a delicious story. Way too long. I'm gonna call the doctor and finish up the invoices unless he can get us in now. I'll text you." She hung up.

Rush leaned against the kitchen door. "He's in his pajamas, TV is on his favorite superhero movie and he's already asleep. Poor kid."

"Thank you. Hailey is calling the doctor. You want coffee?"

"No," he said. "Dispatch called. Semi jackknifed. Hazardous material. I have to go. I hate to jerk him out of bed again to take you to the resort."

"I'll be okay. Besides, Hailey will be here soon to take Dalton to the doctor and I'll ride along for moral support." She gave him an encouraging smile. "I'll be fine. You be careful out there, though."

"Always." He gently clipped her chin with his knuckles. "Lock the door behind me, please."

Nora walked him to the door and watched him get inside his vehicle, then she closed her door and locked it. Coffee didn't sound as good as tea. Calming tea to soothe her nerves.

She headed into the kitchen, straight into a dark-clad figure.

TWELVE

Nora froze at the sight of the man standing in the kitchen, dressed head to toe in black. He came at her and it jerked her into motion.

She pivoted and ran from the kitchen into the living room, heading for the front door. Not to escape but to lure him out of the house and away from Dalton.

Reaching the sofa, he tackled her and they crashed on top of the coffee table, knocking magazines and a vase of flowers to the floor. A searing pain shot up her back, already sore from the car accident.

He shoved her face into the rug as he sat on her back like a weight. She struggled for the crystal vase as the attacker's hands wrapped around her throat and squeezed.

She got her fingers around a broken section and stabbed it into her assailant's gloved hand gripping her throat.

He howled as she ripped through the material, hitting flesh, and he released his grip. She slashed his other gloved hand. Managing to wiggle out from under him, she shot to her feet and raced to the front door. She couldn't leave him here alone with Dalton. Couldn't stay in the house with the child upstairs.

She paused and faced him.

"Is that all you got? Because you're going to have to put me in a snowy grave to stop me!" Hoping her false bravado didn't show the real fear burning through her, she looked her attacker dead in his dark eyes. Dark eyes!

He pulled a hunting knife and acid lurched into her throat. He bounded toward her like she'd intended but now this plan seemed futile. She slid across the porch, leaped down the steps to avoid ice, jarring her back and feeling every move in her stiff muscles. Bolting through the snow, Nora pressed toward the tree line. If she could get into the thatch of woods, she might be able to lose him, and once she broke through to the other side, the resort and lodge wouldn't be that far off. The stables were close and sleigh rides would be in full swing. Someone would see her. Help her.

But she had to make it there first.

Mr. Dressed In Black was hot on her heels and wielding a really big knife.

Wind whipped and stung her face, her lungs burned from gulping eight-degree air. Adrenaline kept her moving, kept her from paying too much attention to the pain in every stride.

She made it to the tree line but tripped over a log and face-planted in a drift of snow. Fighting to get up, she stumbled again and righted herself, barely dodging her attacker.

Screaming for help and continuing to zigzag through the evergreens, Nora felt the man closing in on her. *God, if You can save me from plummeting over the side of a mountain, You can rescue me now and keep Dalton safe!*

Hopefully, her prayers would be heard. Hanging a sharp right, she slipped between the narrow trees, squeezing through. He might have to go an alternate route and if so, Nora would make it to safety.

Ella Fitzgerald crooned, "Sleigh Ride" on the wintry air. She was close to the stable. She could taste freedom.

A hand grabbed the back of her shirt and pulled her to the ground so hard she bit her tongue.

He raised the knife.

She grabbed a gnarly branch.

As he brought it down, she whacked him in the head.

The knife fell from his grasp and he toppled over, unmoving.

She hadn't knocked him out, only stunned him.

Move. Move. Move. Nora forced her exhausted, protesting body to get up and get going. Before she bolted, she grabbed the knife, then fled for safety at Pine Refuge.

Tourists laughed as they imbibed hot cocoa, listened to Christmas carols and climbed into sleighs with quilts and foot warmers, never once realizing a woman had been screaming and running for her life in the woods only yards from them.

She made it to the stable and stumbled inside. A phone on the wall would give her a direct line to Dad's office. Picking it up, she rang him.

"Yes," Dad said.

"Daddy. Daddy, it's me. Come..." She dropped the phone and collapsed on the stable floor. When she awoke, she was in her bed at the chalet and Dad was sitting beside her. Rush stood behind him, worry in his eyes.

"Hey, hon. How do you feel?"

Confused. Exhausted. Hanging by one little thread. "Dalton?" she asked, her throat gritty.

"He's fine." Rush handed her a cup of water that was on the nightstand. "Here, drink this."

She accepted it, feeling the warmth of his fingers discreetly brushing hers and giving her security. "What happened?" The last thing she remembered was calling Dad from the stable phone.

Dad patted her leg. "You called me and said, 'Come,' then the line went dead. I ran out to the stable and found you passed out. John was with you."

The stable hand.

"You had a knife and blood on your hand. I sent John to Dalton. Brought you here."

Nora scooted up in bed and sipped her water again. "Someone was in the kitchen, Rush. When you left I went to make tea and he was there." She finished telling them what happened and how she led the attacker away from the house to protect Dalton. "I'm so sorry. I shouldn't have come back to the main house. I should have brought Dalton to the offices—"

"He's safe. You were very brave, hon. And Hailey is grateful. She's with Dalton right now."

Grateful? She ought to be fuming. Nora had inadvertently put her nephew in danger. "I didn't see his whole face, but his eyes were dark."

"Good. That's good," Rush murmured.

"Ward McKay has dark eyes. Troy Parsons has dark eyes too," she said.

"Troy Parsons?" Dad asked and looked at Rush. "What is going on?"

Rush frowned. "A lot of men have dark eyes. Your dad for one, and do you think he attacked you? Let's not go off half-cocked again just yet."

"Why would Troy Parsons want to hurt Nora?" Joshua asked.

Rush scowled again, then gave Nora a "now what are you going to do" look.

How to explain? Nora was going to have to wound her

father. She should have kept her mouth shut and not been so open with her opinion like Rush had been insisting.

"He...he was seen meeting with Mom a few times before she disappeared. At Mac's."

Dad's eyes narrowed. "Hmm..." Standing, he shook Rush's hand. "Keep me abreast of the situation, Rush. And keep my baby safe." He stalked out of the room, blinking too fast and nostrils flaring.

"You see why I'm careful with my words, Nora? Now he has that image along with so many others to battle through."

Nora closed her eyes. "I'm exhausted, and I should have thought first, spoke second."

Rush sighed and sat on the side of the bed, taking her hand and kissing her knuckles. "Nora, you could have been killed."

"While you were called away by Troy. Convenient."

"Possibly. But we don't know for sure."

She wasn't up for another argument. "Give me my laptop. I need to finish my weather research."

"Right now, you're going to sleep, and I'm going to keep watch. End of story."

He had the no-nonsense face her dad used to have when she asked to go somewhere that wasn't going to bring anything good. "Fine."

Rush eyed her, suspicious.

"What? I said I'd sleep. I'll sleep," she insisted.

His smirk was like a tickle to her ribs, and she grinned. "If I come back in here and you're not sleeping..."

"You'll what?" she flirted. After all that had happened and knowing they were a lost cause, she couldn't help it.

His smirk slid into a full-on lady-killer grin. "I'll—" he seemed to be hunting for a punishment that might fit the crime "—be disappointed."

She half laughed. "I've been living with disappointment most of my life, Rush. You can't scare me."

He leaned in as if he were going to kiss her. His lips were mere inches from hers, his hands resting on either side of the fluffy pillow she was propped up on. Panic sent her heart thrumming. He searched her eyes. "You look scared right now."

She swallowed, couldn't find her voice.

His warm, minty breath filled her senses with anticipation and a heavy dose of alarm. If he kissed her again she'd never recover.

"If I come back in here, Nora Beth, and catch you doing anything but sawing logs…" His eyes revealed exactly what he'd do, what he wanted to do right this second. He slowly came closer. One pucker and they'd make contact. "Just give me a reason," he whispered.

Her brain screamed, "Run." Her heart shouted, "Do it! Kiss me!"

"You'd regret it," she murmured back.

"Probably, but not until it was too late to take it back."

This was not the way to make her sleep. This was a great way to keep her awake for days! Months. Years. It wasn't only that Rush was an amazing kisser; he'd had years to practice it to perfection on her. They'd been each other's first kiss.

This felt like a first kiss kind of anticipation mixed with a measure of fear and excitement. It would do wild things to her physically, but what had her stomach in butterflies was what she'd feel emotionally. The way Rush would pour out his love and affection for her. Like he had so many times before. It had made her feel like she could be anyone. Do anything. That she was his alone. Those kisses had been full of beauty and promise.

Right now, something crackled between them. More

than attraction. Enough to make her want to cry. Hope mixed with the tragic reality that they no longer had hope for a future and it was surely the only thing suspending Rush from dipping lower and exploring her lips.

It would be excruciating on them both when she left. Rush would have to deal with the heartache of watching her leave again—he'd said it himself. But he seemed willing to risk the pain of the future for the joy of the present.

A kiss wouldn't last. It would be over too soon, and they'd be met with waves of confusion. She was already confused enough. Rush loved her. She loved Rush. And love—well love wasn't enough to hold them together. It never had been.

"We were good at this once," Rush whispered.

"We were, but we weren't good at the rest of it." She wasn't good at the rest of it. Opening up. Sticking around when things got tough. "I wasn't. I'll own up to that. I may never be." She knew she needed a change. But she'd run and cocooned herself for so long, she wasn't sure change could be made. And she refused to hurt Rush in the trying process.

His cloudy brown eyes cleared and pain pulsed in them. He tipped up his lips and gently placed a kiss on her forehead. "Get some sleep."

Yeah, right.

He turned at the door. "I'm sorry, Nora. Knowing you were out there being chased by a man with a knife…in the cold. Alone. You could have died and I…I lost it because I can't imagine a world where you're not in it. Even if you're not with me…I want you around for a long time." Emotion clogged his voice, and tears bloomed in her eyes. She didn't have anything but a nod in her.

He quietly closed the door. When she was sure he was in the kitchen and not coming back, she snatched her laptop and powered it up. She had a few weather sites she needed to browse and sleep was not going to happen no matter what he said, or how hard she tried.

Rush collapsed on the couch, staring out the window as the snow fell, leaving a fresh, untouched surface. A clean slate. Any mud, tracks, divots had all been covered with a sheet of white as if nothing lay beneath it. Nothing dark, nothing muddy.

Like God's mercy.

New every morning.

And yet they all lived as though there was none. As if their own lives weren't like fresh fallen snow, pure and white each and every morning they woke. Dad still hung on to his guilt for mistakenly accusing Randy of soliciting. Nora still clung to the belief that she couldn't truly be herself to be loved wholly. Rush's love hadn't been enough to convince her. *God, may Your love do that. Please open her eyes to see that there's nowhere she can go, nothing she can do that will keep You from loving her.*

What about Rush? Was he showing mercy? Man's mercy—yes. The kind where Rush offered enough to make things civil between him and Nora, but that was it. He hadn't forgotten how much heartache Nora had inflicted in the past. He wouldn't attempt to ask for a chance at something new. He couldn't risk it. But how was that new mercy? How was that fresh grace like new snow? His grace, his mercy still had faint footprints of pain, reminding him that it could only be doled out in small measures.

Did that mean he was being cautious or fearful?

Did that mean he wasn't trusting God with his heart? Was he leaving whether he found joy or sorrow up to Nora—up to himself?

He wasn't sure, and he didn't want to dig further or allow God to reveal any truths. If Rush let God do that, he'd be responsible for working through it. And Rush wasn't ready to deal with working through his feelings for Nora. He wished it would stop snowing. That he wouldn't have to keep seeing it laid fresh. That he wouldn't have to fight tooth and nail to keep his heart safe.

Everything was piling up. Work. Troy's possible involvement. A relentless killer bent on shutting Nora up for life. Did this guy realize if he murdered Nora, Rush would never stop coming after him? He'd make it his life's mission to find him and put him away until he stopped breathing. Did this killer think he was so cunning that Rush wouldn't find him? That he would get away scot-free? Because he wouldn't.

Rush glanced at Nora's bedroom door. He didn't for one second think she was sleeping. No, she was probably on the internet right this moment searching past weather conditions and digging around social media sites for clues. But he couldn't go in there. He'd told her what would happen if he did.

And he'd follow through if he walked in there.

Rush would kiss her, pour out his heart, and it would hurt because she'd pour hers right back. She could never withhold her feelings from him—not in a kiss. Thinking about it was only going to drive him mad.

He jumped up and put more wood on the fire, the wood smoke comforting him some. The flames warming him, but only so far. A knock on the door came. He drew his piece and looked out the window.

Troy.

The last person he wanted to see. But the one person he needed to see most. Rush was afraid of the truth. Afraid that another mentor and man he considered a father would disappoint him. Nora said she'd been disappointed so much she was used to it. So was Rush. But he didn't want disappointment to be the norm. Didn't want to expect everyone and everything to let him down. That was no way to live. But to choose the other meant exposing himself and being vulnerable.

Rush holstered his weapon and opened the door. "Troy. What are you doing here?"

"I heard what happened to Nora. Thought I'd come by and check on her. On you." He peeked inside. "Can I come in?"

"Sure." He motioned Troy inside. "Have a seat."

Troy looked around. "I've never been to the chalets before."

"They're state-of-the-art," Rush said.

Sitting on a wingback chair by the hearth, Troy leaned forward. "What can you tell me about what happened? Did she see who did it?"

Rush wasn't sure if Troy was asking as a concerned friend, the sheriff or someone working against them. "He was wearing all black, including a ski mask." Did he tell Troy about the knife? The attacker was wearing gloves but they might be able to get prints. He hated not knowing if he could trust this man. If he accused him of sinister things, Rush would not only lose Troy's endorsement for his run for sheriff, he'd lose a friend and mentor.

But he had to know.

"Troy, did you have any kind of relationship with Marilyn that you might not want to admit?" Rush's stomach knotted.

Troy's bushy eyebrows rose, and then he frowned. "Are you asking me if I betrayed my wife of thirty-two years? If I put my family at risk of falling apart over a fling with a woman who had flings with just about anyone? You really want to ask me that?"

Rush sighed. "I don't want to believe it. But I have to ask. Because the manager at Mac's said he saw you in there with Marilyn on a few occasions before the masquerade ball. It's my duty to follow up."

The sheriff rolled his signature toothpick around his lips. "I didn't have an affair with Marilyn Livingstone. You have my word on that. I love Betty. I'd never do anything to hurt her or Dan."

Troy held Rush's gaze. The chalet was quiet except for the wind outside and firewood popping in the fireplace. Rush wanted to believe him. "Then what were you meeting with Marilyn about?"

Sighing, Troy stood. "I wasn't. The only thing I'm guilty of is going out of town to have a beer. That's my only betrayal where Betty is concerned. Her father was an alcoholic, and she didn't want me having a drink. Not even one beer after a rough day, but some days...some days called for an ice-cold glass of relaxation. I'd go to Mac's and have it."

"And Marilyn?"

"Marilyn was there often. Did I ever sit down and chat with her? Yes, because she was actually a nice person, and she didn't judge me sneaking around to have a drink, but then why would she? She was there sneaking around, I suspect, too. I saw her a few times with Ward McKay. But that wasn't new information."

Rush wanted desperately to trust Troy's explanation. "Then why did the manager say you were with her?"

"I was. Sitting at a table for a while. I suppose like other men who met her there. But I promise nothing untoward happened, and I was probably wrong to do it. Clearly, it gave the impression I was one of her side-suitors. I wasn't. Marilyn wasn't a pariah. I don't know what she was or why she stepped out on Joshua so often."

Troy driving up after they went off a cliff had to be co-incidence. He'd done nothing to thwart the investigation. It made sense not to put all their manpower into investigating what the coroner had signed off on as an accident. If Rush were sheriff, he would have done the same thing.

"Nora has been working on the past weather reports and it's looking like it wasn't wet, snowy or even icy that night. But you remembered it raining and snowing."

"Are you accusing me of something, Rush?" His voice held a hint of anger but mostly surprise and a splash of hurt and offense.

"No. Just trying to get answers."

"I do remember it raining and snowing that night, late, not during the party. But it was seventeen years ago. I barely remember what I ate for breakfast yesterday. I could be wrong. I'm not saying I can't. But that doesn't mean I'm lying on purpose. And to a woman I know is a forensic meteorologist and could prove me wrong or right? Why would I do that?"

Why indeed?

Nora's paranoid suspicions were messing with his head. Troy wasn't guilty of murder or attempted murder. "Do you think Ward McKay could be behind these attacks on Nora? Him or Harvey Langston?"

"I don't like Harvey for it."

"When Nora was attacked at the hotel, Ward was with me."

"Doesn't mean Ward didn't have someone do him a favor. I wouldn't put anything past him. He's double-dealing in business. Why not in his personal life as well? But I stand by my call and the coroner's. If he's after Nora for digging into the past it's not because he hurt Marilyn. Could be about that money, though."

"Why would Marilyn take him that kind of money? And since she never gave it to him, it's dead in the water, pardon the pun. Why come after Nora now? What could she dig up—with my help—that would expose him?"

Troy held his toothpick and used it to point at Rush. "That's the million-dollar question, son. I'd do a little hunting around his business deals. But if that's where the answers lie, then expect even more backlash. And be discreet."

He could count on that. "I'm sorry, Troy, if it seemed like I was interrogating you—"

"Seemed?" His eyebrows twitched skyward. "Hey, it's good work. You'll make a mighty fine sheriff, Rush. I've always thought so. You don't need my endorsement to beat out Jack Thomas, or anyone." He hugged him, clapping him on the back.

"You heading back to the station?" Rush asked.

"I am. Whatcha need?"

Rush lifted his coat off the table and took the gallon freezer bag holding the serrated knife. Nora had cut the attacker and it had some blood on it. Possibly prints. "He came at Nora with this. She cut up his hands and there's some blood. Can you enter it and get it to the lab? I don't want to leave her."

Troy accepted the bag, inspected the knife. "Hunting knife. Not uncommon. Good thing Nora's quick. She may not have made it, and this would be an entirely different conversation."

"Agreed." He was beyond thankful for God's protection of Nora.

Troy headed for the door, turned back. "Give her my

best, though I doubt she wants it if she's labeled me a criminal."

"She's confused."

"I'll keep you posted." With that, he closed the door. The lights flickered. The power had been going on and off for days.

He walked to Nora's door and knocked, giving her time to put that laptop away and pretend sleep, ultimately giving her and himself an out.

"Nora," he called. Maybe she was asleep. He cracked the door and saw her lying on her side. He walked in and noticed the laptop on the floor. Touching it, he felt the warmth.

Faker. He grinned but went along with the facade. "Wake up, Nora Beth. We gotta talk."

Now to make her believe that Troy wasn't the enemy.

But someone was. He'd been brazen enough to get into the main house. He was desperate and reckless.

And that meant unstable.

Unstable meant unpredictable.

Unpredictable meant Rush was at a disadvantage, and that terrified him.

THIRTEEN

It was already Christmas Eve and Nora hadn't even thought about a ball gown or masquerade mask. Seemed like a silly event to attend when someone was trying to kill her, but Rush had insisted on some normalcy—not to mention he had to be at the ball.

She stood inside Hailey's room staring at the gowns lying across her bed.

"Pick any one you like. I should have put them in consignment, but I figured I'd recycle them. Glad I did." Hailey sat on an empty space on the bed that wasn't covered with sequins, silk and satin. "I'm behind on the event since Dalton's been sick."

"Hey, at least it wasn't the flu." Two days and his fever had broken. He was still a bit lethargic, but his appetite had returned with a vengeance and he would be well enough to stay with Nathan tonight.

"Yeah. It's going to be weird not having him at all on Christmas Eve. We used to bake cookies and open one present that day, then come to the ball. I suppose he and Nate will go to his parents'. They never liked the ball anyway." Hailey shrugged and held up a strapless red silky dress with a large red sash and a rhinestone pendant on the side. It was gorgeous. "I think you should wear this one." She rummaged through the pile on the bed. "And this mask."

A black-and-gold mask on a gold stick. Ornate. Touch of glitter for shine. Classy and elegant. "Okay. I like it." Red and Christmassy. "Now that my costume is picked out, how can I help you catch up?"

"It's mostly overseeing what's going on in the ballroom. Ice sculptures, caterers, decorators. Sound guys are supposed to be here at two for a sound check." She sighed. "I need the crew to come back through and shovel the snow from the chalet drives and roads leading up to the resort, and the parking lot."

Nora peered out the window. It had been coming down hard all morning. "I don't think it'll do any good, sis. The overnight temps were low with high relative humidity and low winds...high pressure system. Black ice is coming. People need to stay indoors and off the roads."

"Nothing is going to keep people from this masquerade ball."

The power flickered.

Died.

"Great," Nora mumbled.

"Generator will kick on in a minute." Hailey checked her cell phone. "I have to get to the resort. And you can't be left alone."

Nora felt like a helpless child.

"I've got the snowmobile. It's easier than trying to deal with a vehicle. Grab your things. I'm gonna call and check on Dalton real quick."

Nora nodded and headed for the kitchen to collect her purse, coat and gloves. Black gloves. Reminded her of the attacker from a few days ago and the knife he'd come at her with. Rush had given that piece of evidence to Troy. Nora hadn't been thrilled to hear about Rush's conversation with Troy, but it did make sense. Why lie about the weather knowing she had the skills to prove him wrong? And she had.

She'd scoured the National Climatic Data Center, co-op sites, which were a notch above Weather Underground but she'd checked there too, collecting what data she could. She'd studied the weather information for that Christmas Eve as well as five days prior and after. In all likelihood, there had been no ice, no black ice. Not even wet roads. Weather was probably not a factor in Mom's accident. Troy may have made a mistake. And Nora was hunting for a culprit to pin this on.

She caught a shadow at the living room window; her heart lurched and she clutched her chest, then exhaled and relaxed. Rush. She opened the door and shivered. The temperature was in single digits. "Hey," she said.

"Hey," he said as breath plumed in front of his face. His nose and cheeks were pink. "It's crazy out there. Northern half of town is shut down. No power. Pipes are frozen in many homes and businesses, meaning no water. It's going to get even worse tonight. I don't think anyone local should be driving."

"Locals won't drive. They'll bring snowmobiles." She laughed. "And freeze in ball gowns and faux fur coats."

The blustery winds rattled the window and whistled. "It's gorgeous, though," she said. Trees looked made of glass. Hints of evergreen peeked through. Nothing but a white winter wonderland.

"I told Mom I'd come by and eat a bite. She can't stand me not being there for festivities, and they're hurrying it up in case they lose power. You mind riding along?" he asked.

"No. I'd like to see Greer again. When is she going back to Alabama?"

"Supposed to be the day after Christmas, but I don't see that happening. Not if we get two inches of ice tonight and another one tomorrow. Weather is calling for it and another two feet of snow."

Nora smirked. "I'm well aware of what the weather is supposed to be doing."

"I suppose you are."

"Hey," Hailey said as she came into the living room, snug as a bug in her winter gear. "I'm leaving. You with me or going with Rush?"

"Rush."

Nora spotted the knowing look. Rush was protecting her. That's all.

"See you tonight?"

"Yeah. But I may have on boots with my gown and not heels."

Hailey snickered. "You'd think bad weather would keep folks away. But Christmas brings people together no matter what storm is raging." Sadness flickered on her face. "Well, most people are brought together."

She hurried out and Rush turned to Nora. "Nathan's a real jerk."

Nora nodded. "Ready?"

Rush guided her outside and into the vehicle.

"We probably shouldn't be out in this either."

Rush started the motor. "Well, I have chains and, hey…we've made it over the mountainside once. We can do it again."

Nora frowned.

"Too soon?"

She laughed. "Little bit."

Inching along the roads, it took almost thirty minutes to arrive at Rush's childhood home. Festive lights wrapped around the porch rails. "Lights are new."

"Hollister was bored I think."

Inside, the fire blazed and Nora welcomed the warmth. The dining room table was still covered in sweets galore and the smell of cinnamon and Christmas ham set her stomach rumbling. Nora loved the Buchanan ham. Cured and cooked for nine hours. She would be up all night gulping water from so much salt intake, but it was worth it. The tree twinkled with colored lights and tinsel. Bing Crosby's "White Christmas" played in the background. Kids ripped and tore through the house and adult laughter helped drown it out.

"Merry Christmas, Nora." Mrs. Buchanan took her coat. "Come in, out of that terrible weather." She pointed at Rush. "You don't need to be driving in this."

"Yes, ma'am." He kissed her cheek. "I can't stay long, Mama."

"You work too hard, and it's Christmas Eve. Eat. Make merry," she teased, and patted his cheek.

Rush was nothing if not a mama's boy at heart.

"Yes, ma'am," he said again, and Mrs. Buchanan bustled away.

"You hungry?" he asked.

"Starving, and I smell Christmas ham."

He chuckled and led her to the kitchen. Hollister leaned against the refrigerator, mischief in his eyes, as they came in. He pointed upward.

Mistletoe.

"Kiss her or I'll come under and do it," he teased.

Rush frowned and glanced up again. "Well, it is tradition."

"It is that," she murmured. And Hollister would make good on his word—the insatiable flirt. The last thing she needed was Rush punching him like he had when they were sixteen.

Her stomach fluttered, and her heart sped up as Rush descended on her lips. Soft. Chaste, but lingering long enough to send a serious zing through her middle.

Hollister opened the fridge and pulled out a soda. "Pitiful, Rush. Pitiful." He cracked open the can, wiggled his eyebrows and strode out of the kitchen.

"I didn't think it was pitiful, Nora Beth. Did you?" His eyes held mischief of their own. "I can try again if you did."

"I—"

"Nora, good to see you again." Pastor Buchanan entered the kitchen, eyed the mistletoe. "Am I interrupting?"

"Not at all, Dad," Rush said, and backed a foot away from Nora.

"Rush, can you bring the card table in from the craft room?" Mrs. Buchanan called.

"Yes, ma'am." He tossed one last glance at the mistletoe and winked at Nora. That was not fair. Not holding up to his words. Words like they could never be together. Rush wasn't one to lead her on. He must be as confused as she was. Her head told her it was futile. Her heart said something else.

"Will you be staying long?" Pastor Buchanan asked.

"No. I took a job in Florida. I leave at the New Year."

"I thought maybe you and Rush might be…" He shrugged, but a hint of amusement danced in his eyes. He seemed more like the man he used to be.

"It's complicated."

He pursed his lips, started to leave, then stopped. "Love usually is."

No one said anything about love. Oh, who was she kidding? "I don't know if we could ever get past our heartbreaks, Pastor Buchanan."

His eyes widened. "It's been a long time since I've been called that."

Nora used to call him that all the time. He had been her pastor. A mentor. A role model. "I don't think one mistake should cost you the honor of being one."

"And one or two mistakes ought not cost you a chance at being with someone you love."

Nora's chest cracked a little. If that were only true. "To be honest, he's made it clear that we're nothing but friends. We have too much bad history. I'm sure you know that."

A flicker of light came into his eyes. "Love covers a multitude of sins, Nora."

"Not sure it covers fast enough to Mach speed racers like me." She swallowed the emotion clogging her throat as it dawned on her. "I suppose you and I are similar."

"How's that?" he asked quietly.

"Hiding away, keeping things inside and not letting anyone in. Rush calls it running—physically and metaphorically. And he's not wrong."

When he looked at her, moisture filled his eyes. "This is why he...why he wants to keep things platonic?"

"It's why he should," she whispered. "I can't promise not to do it again."

Pastor Buchanan looked longingly into the living room; more moisture sheened his eyes and he wiped them. Slowly, he turned. "Love does cover a multitude of sins. It reaches far and wide. And fast, Nora. Love moves fast when it needs to." He glanced back at his wife and sucked his trembling bottom lip into his mouth. "The question is, do we let it blanket us or do we stand out in the cold and keep shivering unnecessarily?"

Was that rhetorical or was he asking himself?

Suddenly, he inhaled and squeezed her shoulder. "Thank you."

For what? She didn't get a chance to ask. Rush came into the kitchen with a card table in his arms. "Where am I supposed to put this?"

"By the laundry room," his mother said. "I know it's early but you're leaving, so will you come and read the Nativity story before you go?"

Pastor Buchanan had always done that in years past. Guess Rush took up the mantle after all that happened. Pastor Buchanan caught Nora's glance. The flicker in his eyes had turned into a bright and shining flame, as if life had suddenly come back into them. He grasped his wife's hand. "I think I'd like to do it."

Tears filled Rush's mom's eyes. "I'd like that, darling."

"Let me get my Bible." He paused next to Nora, kissed her cheek. "Thank you, dear one." Then he disappeared into the living room.

Rush gaped. "What just happened?"

Nora wasn't sure. "I don't know."

Dad hadn't read the Nativity story since he lost the church. Now Nora waltzed into the house and, all of a sudden, he was offering to go and get his Bible and read it aloud? Rush hadn't seen his dad with the worn, black leather-bound Good Book in ages. She had to have done something. His father had thanked her!

"Well," his mother said, "I don't know either, but I'm thanking you also." She patted Nora's cheek and left Rush alone with her.

"What did you talk about?"

"Complications. And love."

Rush cupped her face. "What about love?"

"That it covers a multitude of sins."

Nora had been believing for something wonderful at Christmas. Was this it? A turning point for Dad?

"Everyone, gather round," his father called.

"Well, whatever you did or didn't do…it shifted something loose in my dad. Come on. Let's hear the story of our Lord's birth."

"I'd like that."

Rush laced his hand in hers and led her to the living room. The reading of the birth of Christ the Lord never failed to move Rush to tears. It reminded him of how frail and flawed he was and how gracious and merciful and loving God was.

Dad finished his reading and paused, then he prayed.

Rush could hardly stand upright. His father. Was praying. For peace. For joy. For hope.

Mom leaned against Dad and cried.

They were witnessing answers to prayers that had been going up for a decade. On this holy eve, God was giving them the greatest gift.

Rush was getting his father back.

Mom was getting her husband back.

What about Rush's prayers? Would they be answered anytime soon? Would he ever find love that would work out, have a family of his own?

After prayer, the family piled plates full of ham, potatoes, casseroles, deviled eggs and homemade yeast rolls. Nora sat beside Greer at the kitchen table, talking and laughing.

"Son, can we talk a minute?"

Rush set his plate on the counter. "Sure." He followed Dad into his study and shut the door.

"I owe you an apology."

"For?"

"The last ten years. And for keeping you from the woman you love."

"Dad, you didn't keep me from Nora. We did that all by ourselves." Rush leaned against the desk and crossed an ankle over the other.

"Fear has kept you from going after her. Fear she's like me. Like what I've become. It's true. I've been wallowing in guilt for what I did, in bitterness for what happened, anger at God for allowing it. I thought I'd lost everything, but I didn't. The most important things to me were still here, still covering me with love, and I ignored it to be selfish. To be resentful and fearful."

Rush swallowed the lump in his throat.

"You see me and what I've done to this family in Nora. For that I'm sorry. Because tonight I saw the love you have for her. And the pain. I've been afraid to live for ten years. Don't be me. Don't think Nora is me."

Dad hugged him hard and tight. "She helped me see that tonight, and it hit me that my son is miserable because of me and I can't have that. Your mother has been miserable because of me."

"Dad, I love you."

"I love you too, son."

"But it doesn't change anything with Nora. She won't confide in me. Open up to me. I can't be with a woman who won't give me all of her heart. All of her dreams and fears and everything. Even if you hadn't changed... I would still feel the same way about her. I would still want it all. And she can't give me that."

Dad nodded. "Love covers a multitude of sins."

But what did that mean? Was Rush to love her and hope she wouldn't leave him again when things got tough? He'd barely recovered from the last time.

"I don't know if love can cover distrust. And I can't

trust her not to leave me when things get rough, and it's no secret marriages aren't perfect. I want someone like Mama."

"I'll pray for you, son."

Rush hadn't heard those words in so long. Tears stung the backs of his eyes. "I'd like that."

"And I suspect you'd like some answers on this case."

Dad may have answers and was willing to help him, to divulge information. This was beyond anything Rush could ever imagine. Proof God had been working to soften him over the years. To bring him to this point. Rush could hardly speak. "I would if you have any. Did you see anyone in the Phantom of the Opera mask that wasn't Harvey Langston or Ward McKay?"

Dad sighed and rubbed the back of his neck. "After I accused Randy of that crime…I promised myself I'd never speak about another person again no matter what. But Nora's life is at stake. And so is yours. I do know of one man who wore a Phantom of the Opera mask that night. And I know he was involved romantically with Marilyn because I witnessed him kissing her the night before, near the lake, when I was on patrol."

Rush couldn't believe his ears. "Why didn't you say anything after she disappeared?"

"Because I promised him as a pastor that I wouldn't. I felt guilty about it, which is why when Randy was in that old pool hall in the woods, I didn't hold back because I'd done it before. I had to be honest."

"Who did you see kissing Marilyn?" It was undoubtedly the same man Rush saw kissing her the next night in the offices.

"Gary Plenk."

The words knocked the breath from him. Gary had been a deacon in Dad's church. But more than that—he was the county coroner. "Is that why he stepped down as a deacon?"

"It was our deal. He stepped down, and if Marilyn returned they would break it off, and I wouldn't say anything to Troy about it. Besides, I never believed for a second he had anything to do with her disappearance. In fact, I thought he might be getting ready to leave his wife and go with her, but when I approached him he was confused. Upset. He didn't know what happened to her. And we made our deal."

Rush's mind reeled. "Thank you for sharing that information. It's helpful. Beyond helpful. I need to find Nora."

"Go on. Be careful."

"I will." He gave him one more hug and found Nora where he left her. Sitting at the table with Greer's baby in her arms. "Hey."

She glanced up and must have read his expression; she passed the baby back to Greer and stood. "Ready?"

"Yeah."

Once they were back inside the Bronco he told her everything his dad shared.

"Rush. What if he was lying about the striations being inconclusive? If he was kissing my mom one minute, and then the next she was leaving town without him…?"

"A fight could have gone down. We can send the reports and photos to a coroner outside the county and get a second opinion. Be sure."

"He's still with his wife. Me digging around might have turned it up—it did turn it up. He has a lot to lose. Besides his reputation."

"His family. His marriage. Before we approach him, let's get that information emailed to someone else."

"Okay. I need to change and get ready for the ball tonight."

"We can do that as soon as I swing by the station and email an outside coroner. I know someone in Shelby County that's a friend."

"Memphis area?"

"Yeah. We went to summer camp together."

The tires rolled over packed snow and ice, and the vehicle rocked. Branches clanked like ice in glasses as the wind hurled through the trees. They slid a few times, Rush righting them, but his face was grim, jaw working.

He pulled up at the station. "Sit tight. I won't be but a minute. No point in us both having to get out and freeze." He left the Bronco running and hurried inside. The station was quiet since most deputies were out helping on the roads, due to downed power lines and car accidents. It was a nightmare out there. He rifled through the box of evidence, scanned the photos and report, then emailed it to Walt Brudebaker. Then he sent him a text telling him he had mail and it was of utmost priority.

Back inside the Bronco, he shivered and turned the heat back up to full blast. "I can't believe we're going to a party."

Nora snorted. "Well, believe it."

"I want coffee by the fire and that's all."

"You'll look good in a tux."

"But I'll be cold."

"My dress is off one shoulder so I don't wanna hear it."

He'd like to see it. And he would in a few hours.

"Are you going to tell Troy about Gary Plenk?"

"As soon as I hear back from Walt. If it is inconclusive, then I'm going to approach Gary with some questions." He didn't want to be the bearer of bad news again, but... "Nora, you have to know that if we don't find some kind of solid evidence or if someone doesn't outright admit they were with her that night and know what that money was for, then we may never know the details."

Nora smeared ChapStick on her lips. "I know. But what if this Walt person says otherwise about the marks on my mother's skull?"

"Then we know Gary has lied and that implicates him in foul play."

"But you still have no hard evidence."

"No." That was the worst part of this. The killer could go free. Yeah, Gary might lose his license. But even if he had a silver cuff link and Phantom of the Opera mask, that was all circumstantial and wouldn't convict him in a court of law. Not of murder in any degree. And no one seemed to know what the money was for and probably never would.

FOURTEEN

Gold and glass-beaded chandeliers hung in rows from the ceiling of the ballroom. Buffet tables with black table-cloths held silver warmers and white china plates rimmed in gold. Savory garlic and onions wafted from the magnificent dishes underneath the heavy lids.

Sparkling cider flowed down a mountain of champagne glasses, creating a beautiful amber waterfall. The center of the room held a Nativity ice sculpture that was breathtaking. The round sitting tables dotting the massive room were covered in black, gold and silver with pops of red. A live band, including a string quartet, was already faintly playing Christmas carols. It was glorious.

Nora had changed and Dad had brought her to the resort to oversee a few things for Hailey so she could dress in her gown.

The twenty-foot fir was trimmed in crystal icicles, glittery ornaments and dazzling gold beads. Nora gazed on it with fond memories. This had been her favorite night growing up. Families would come and dine together, then staff took children under twelve back to the kids' corner, where they watched Christmas movies, made crafts, ate cookies and drank cocoa until parents arrived for them before midnight. At midnight, masks would be removed and everyone sang, "We Wish You a Merry Christmas" with the band and toasted Christmas morning in.

Nora couldn't stay in Splendor Pines, but she had to admit she didn't want to go. She had no job here. Debt to pay.

And there was Rush. Staying was too hard. But maybe there was a way.

A throat cleared and drew her attention from the band and the tree.

Rush stood at the doorway in a black tux, black vest and tie. He'd never been a fan of bow ties. The gold flecks in his hair were magnified by the twinkling lights in the chandeliers. He'd shaved, and a dimple on his left cheek was visible. Broad shoulders carried that jacket well. But the black mask with pewter designs brought out his amber eyes. Her mouth turned dry.

He swaggered toward her. When he reached her, he gave her an admiring appraisal. "You look amazing," he murmured.

She held her mask over her eyes. "Oh, this old thing," she teased, and snickered, but his open approval of her appearance did wild numbers on her heart.

He held out his hand and motioned with his chin to the string quartet practicing. "Can I have the first unofficial dance of the night?"

The first. The last.

Would he want her to be his last dance? She curtsied, and he chuckled and took her hand in his, guiding her against him and placing his other hand on her upper back, drawing their intertwined fingers to his chest. Then he glided her across the floor in a waltz like a contender in one of those reality dancing TV shows. "Been practicing, have you?" she asked.

"Maybe. Or maybe I remember those horrid dance classes my mother made me go to before I was stuck escorting Greer to her cotillion."

"You'd think 'coming out' parties would have been banned long ago due to women's rights efforts."

"Some things never go out down South. You know this." He turned her effortlessly and grinned. "Did I mention you look amazing?"

"I don't think you did," she teased.

"My apologies. You look amazing." His lips met her ear. "You smell amazing too."

His breath tickled her sides.

"You look quite handsome yourself."

He drew her closer as they danced in front of the Christmas tree to the sounds of violins, viola and cello playing the "Christmas Waltz."

Could they possibly be more? Have a fresh start? Even with a killer out for blood and finding out she wasn't Dad's biological daughter—in all that mess and pain, for once in a long time she felt hope. Dinner at Rush's, seeing his father read the Bible and pray had done something. God hadn't given up on Rush's dad. Even when he'd turned his back on God. Finally, the hope and love had broken through.

Could it also break through for Nora? For Rush?

"Rush?"

"Yes," he said and gazed into her eyes.

"What if I didn't go to Florida? What if I stayed here?"

He faltered in his perfect dance steps. "Are you being serious right now?"

"Yeah. I could...I don't know...find work." Somewhere. Somehow. "Spend more time with Hailey—be here for her while she goes through this tough time. Be here for Dalton. Help with the resort, even." It was the family business. "And...then there's us."

"Us," he murmured. "I—I want you to stay. If you want to stay. But..."

Nothing about his earlier words had changed. His dad's breakthrough hadn't reached him. He didn't feel the same hope as Nora, and the rejection slid into her lungs, deflating them like a popped balloon. A balloon full of hope. "You know what? It was just a thought." Humiliation racked her every nerve.

"Nora, I—" His phone rang.

"Better take that." She slipped from his embrace and scurried through the tables. She needed some time to compose herself. She beelined it to the elevator and took it down to the offices. Inside Dad's office, she laid her handbag on the desk and slumped in his chair and cried.

The case was closed. Rush's hesitation, his lack of enthusiasm, said it all. He didn't trust her. Didn't want her. Had all this investigation on her mother shown him the probability of what his future might look like? She wiped her eyes, leaving trails of mascara on her hands. The last thing she needed was guests and Rush seeing she'd been crying. Seeing she was heartbroken.

She hurried to the office entrances and was met by Harrison on the golf cart. "I need a ride! To the main house." She slid in with Harrison.

"Everything okay?" he asked and sped up.

"No, it's not." Nothing felt okay. She'd made an attempt to change, to open up like Rush had wanted, and he'd shut her down.

Harrison pulled up to the house. "Be careful, Nora. Weather ain't gonna get no better."

"Thanks for the ride." She froze. She'd forgotten her keys. Her purse was in Dad's office. "Wait! Harrison! Do you have a set of spare keys on you?" He'd been there in a pinch several times over the years when Nora or Hailey had locked themselves out.

"Some things don't change, Nora." He chuckled and unlocked the front door. "If you need a ride back, call the security line."

"Thank you." She shivered and entered the house, then switched on the light.

Nothing but darkness.

The generator must have run out of gas or something. Suddenly, the darkness crept up her spine, leaving cold chills. With her hands stretched out in front of her to guide the way, she maneuvered through the living room and down the hall to her old childhood room. Once inside, she dug through the nightstand drawer and found a battery-operated Christmas candle. She turned the plastic flame and brought a tiny orange glow to the room.

Now what? What did she do next?

She collapsed on her bed; her hand hit something soft and silky. Sitting up, she squinted in the dark and raised the pitiful candle.

Her mouth fell open and the scream rising from her gut wouldn't make its way from her lips.

Hailey lay next to her, in her evening gown and masquerade mask.

Blood covered the bed.

Covered Hailey's middle.

Hailey didn't move. Her chest didn't seem to be rising and falling with breath.

"Nooo!" She felt for a pulse, didn't find one. She picked up the receiver on the phone by the bed but there was no dial tone. Power lines must be down. Her phone was in her purse in Dad's office.

Tilting Hailey's chin back, she began CPR. Every muscle in her body shook; her lips trembled.

This was all her fault. Someone had mistaken Hailey in her mask and gown for Nora and put a bullet in her.

Please, breathe, Hailey.

In this moment, she wished she had listened and stayed out of it. Rush and Hailey were right. There might never be answers and the ones that came would have emotional and physical consequences. Nora had ignored it all for the need to feel loved and not abandoned by Mom.

But wasn't that exactly what had happened that night? Mom was deserting them. She might have come back like other times.

Or she might not have.

Hot tears slicked down Nora's cheeks until they turned to sobs. "God, please! Please!" She repeated it over and over.

How would Nora tell Dalton that his mama was dead, and it was all Nora's fault?

"Please!"

One and two and…

Breathe. Breathe.

And one and two and…

Rush pinched the bridge of his nose. He'd just hung up with Troy. Another car pileup had occurred and the power was now out on most of the south side of town too. But more important, once again, Nora had taken off. And that's why he'd hesitated when she'd brought up them as a couple and her staying. Nothing would make him happier than to be with Nora and live right here in Splendor Pines. But she wouldn't even wait around to have an adult conversation about why he'd paused.

She'd taken his words as complete rejection and instead of listening, she let her assumptions send her out into the night where it wasn't safe. They needed some space and air, but with a killer out there, she should have waited until he was off the phone. But she'd taken advantage of his need to be on that call and thrown all caution to the wind. Did she not care one iota what it might to do him?

No. She didn't think about anyone but herself sometimes. Like now. And as much air and space as Rush needed away from Nora to think things through, he couldn't give it to her because he couldn't leave her alone. He'd already searched the main hall and offices, calling out her name. She wasn't on the property.

Without her car, she wouldn't have gone far. Security was on golf carts. She probably caught a ride to the main house. Or the chalet. Both dumb ideas with everything going on.

His phone rang.

Walt, his coroner friend.

"Hey, Walt." Rush hunched in the weather and dashed for his vehicle.

"I know it's Christmas Eve but it didn't take long to look at those photos and come to a conclusion."

Rush hopped inside his truck. "And what conclusion is that?"

"It's clear that Marilyn Livingstone was murdered."

Faltering to get the keys in the ignition, Rush paused. "Say that again. How so?"

"I don't know why it wasn't ruled a homicide."

Rush had a few ideas. Gary Plenk. Where. Was. Nora? Rush's blood turned to ice.

"Go on," he said, and cranked the engine. *Please let her be at the main house or the chalet.*

He could barely swallow, barely hear Walt speaking.

"The markings on her skull have indentions that match a crowbar perfectly—if you know what to look for, which I do. Someone hit her, and hard enough to leave those impressions in the bone."

Sliding on the ice, he tightened his grip on the steering wheel and made his way down the road that cut up to the main house. The snow fell in fat flakes like white ash from a volcano. "Would she have been alive long enough to drive a car into the lake?"

That at least had to have been an accident—otherwise someone had thought their tracks were covered. No wonder someone was bent on killing Nora. They'd never expected to have that car found. Gary hadn't expected that. But he was in a prime position to lie. He knew Rush would look at that report. See the indentations, not be able to identify it as a layperson and therefore putting all his trust in Gary's lie.

"No. That kind of blow would cause immediate death. If her car was found in the lake with her in it, then it was put there after the blow to the head."

"Walt, thank you for getting back to me so quickly. Merry…Merry Christmas," he mumbled, and hung up as he pulled into the drive at the main house.

Gary Plenk had mountains to lose back then and now.

Rush bounded up the steps to a wide-open front door; his knees turned to water and his heart jumped into his throat. He grabbed his flashlight, drew his weapon and raced inside. No sign of a struggle. He ran down the hall and into Nora's bedroom.

Was that— Was she—

As he came closer he realized the dress wasn't red, but black.

The hair a darker blond and longer.

Hailey.

Blood.

Where was Nora? He checked Hailey's pulse.

Faint. But there. He used his cell phone and called it in. Gunshot wound to the abdomen.

"Hang on, Hailey. We're gonna get you help." But where was Nora? Had the killer shot Hailey and abducted Nora? Had she even been here at all?

Or did the killer mistake Hailey for Nora in the dark?

"Rush?"

"Back here, Troy."

Troy entered. "Just got back from the pileup. Drove by. Saw your vehicle and the door wide-open. What happened? Where's Nora?"

"I don't know. Nora took off about thirty minutes ago. I came looking for her. I found Hailey like this. Could you check the chalet for me? I'll stay here with Hailey."

And hope she didn't die. Hope that Nora was out there and safe.

Nora entered the ballroom as the power died. She'd thrown on boots and run through the snow and ice to the party to get help for Hailey. Throngs of people gasped and moaned and groaned over the inconvenience of the power outage. Candlelight from the tables illuminated the rooms. Why wasn't the generator on? Where was Dad?

Hailey needed medical attention, but Nora feared she was already dead. She had no pulse that Nora could find.

Nora pushed through the people, looking for Rush or Troy. Someone who might be able to help her, but she couldn't find anyone. Her mind raced as panic took over.

Her purse was in the office. She'd get her phone and call Rush. Call 911. Something! Anything! She hated leaving Hailey there all alone and bleeding, but she also had to get some kind of help.

She headed for the stairwell leading to the offices. As she opened the door to the stairs, a hand grabbed hers. Dan stood dressed in his tux. "I've been looking for you."

"Dan, I don't have time to talk right now. Hailey's... Hey, is your dad here? Do you have a radio by any chance?"

His eyes clouded over and he seemed to be agitated. "Dad? No... I mean yes, he's... Nora, we have to talk."

"Fine, but talk fast." She bounded down the stairs, Dan right behind. "What's going on?" She raced for Dad's office.

Inside, she flipped on the light out of habit. No power. Only a trace of moonlight filtering through the windows. Dan grabbed her arm.

"Hey!" she yelled. "What is wrong with you?"

Dan's face turned eerie in the low light. Nora got a sick feeling in her gut. "Nothing. It's... I...I have to talk... I'm..."

"Dan, you're scaring me. Let go of my arm. Right now."

The lights flickered.

Flickered again.

Stayed on! Landlines might be working now. She grabbed the phone and Dan yanked it from her, slamming it back on the cradle. "I need to talk to you! Are you not hearing me?"

Sweat slicked Dan's face; his glazed eyes darted around the room.

All Nora wanted was to get help for Hailey. "Dan, my sister is hurt. I need to call in some help." She held her hands up, every bone in her body trembling. "Calm down. We can figure this out."

"That's the problem, Nora. You have to try to figure

everything out." His eyes darkened and he stepped toward her. Fear iced her heart. "Why did you have to go digging into your mom's death?"

FIFTEEN

Rush held pressure on Hailey's wound and prayed she would make it. This was his fault. If he'd sped up the investigative process like Nora wanted, if he'd pressed Dad for information like she'd asked sooner and more often, they might have found out about Gary Plenk earlier. But he hadn't. He'd been too afraid of stepping on toes and making mistakes. How would Nora ever forgive him for this?

"Hang in there, Hailey. You have a little boy that won't be ready to see his mama go. Fight."

Sirens signaled the arrival of ambulances and Troy bounded into the bedroom. "No sign of her in the chalet, Rush."

Either she'd been taken or… He couldn't think of what might be the worst-case scenario. "By any chance have you been up to the ball?"

"Earlier, why?"

"Did you happen to see Gary Plenk?" *Hang in there, Hailey.* She was too pale. Too still.

"Saw his wife, so I assume he's up there. Why? You want to call him down here or something?" Troy glanced toward the front of the house as the sirens grew louder.

"No." His dread grew. Gary was here. He had access to Nora. "He doctored the death certificate, and he might have Nora right now. Hired someone to take her—hurt her."

Troy's eyes narrowed. "And how would you know that? You talk to him? He admit it?"

"No. I found out before I arrived. I sent the report to a friend in Shelby County."

First responders entered the house. Rush stepped aside and let them do their job. Fear coursed through his veins. Putting her on a gurney, they took her from the home.

"Why would you do that?"

"Because Nora still wasn't sold on the fact that you aren't the one coming after her." Rush's cheeks heated even saying it.

"Nora or you?" Troy demanded.

Rush shook his head. Right now, all that mattered was Nora. "Put a BOLO out for Plenk."

"And what if he's not the man who has her? You put out a BOLO, people are gonna talk."

"Let them talk." Rush wasn't going to let his fear interrupt his job or stop him from finding the only woman he'd ever loved ever again. "I'm heading up to the ball. Call it in, Troy. Now."

Troy licked his upper lip.

"Troy, what is it? I don't have time. Nora could die!"

Raking a hand through his hair, Troy dropped his head. "Gary Plenk did doctor those records."

Troy knew? "Why didn't you say something?"

He raised his head, met Rush's eyes and nothing but shame filled them. "Because I told him to do it, or I'd expose the fact that he'd had an affair with Marilyn."

Rush felt the weight of his words, the betrayal, and it knocked him back a step. "Why?" It made no sense. Unless Troy had lied and did have an affair with Marilyn. Had he seen her kissing Gary Plenk that night and killed her? "What did you do, Troy?" He slowly placed his hand on his holster. "And where is Nora?"

"Don't go getting trigger-happy, Rush." Troy held up his hands. "I didn't hurt Marilyn."

"But you were having an affair with her. You lied." And he hadn't responded to the question about Nora. It was a like a nest of merciless wasps had descended on him.

"I didn't lie. I never had an affair with her, but I knew the truth about her. She'd had too much to drink one night at Mac's and she'd been crying. She told me she had escaped from a man who wanted her dead. Sometimes she got scared and bailed, but she always came back. I told her I could help her, but she clammed up. That night at the Christmas Eve Masquerade Ball I went to talk to her about it again. I found her in the office."

"With Gary Plenk?"

"No. Alone. She was crying."

Before or after Rush spotted her kissing Gary?

"So what happened?"

"I hugged her. Told her whatever had happened would be okay and that it was time for her to come clean about everything, that I'd help her. She promised to come see me the day after Christmas. But she vanished."

"Why blackmail Gary then, Troy? Why didn't you tell what you knew about Marilyn back then...or in this investigation? You never even tried to find the man you thought was after her?" Which was Scott Rhodes. "How could you? They have the right to know that Marilyn was murdered. And where. Is. Nora?"

"Because I was protecting my son, Rush."

Protecting Dan?

Troy's eyes brimmed with tears. "He made a mistake,

Rush. That's all, and I couldn't let it ruin his life forever. What kind of dad would that make me?"

Rush's blood turned cold. "What kind of mistake?"

"That night, he caught me embracing Marilyn in the office. He got the wrong idea and instead of confronting me, he followed Marilyn. Confronted her at the lake. They got into a heated argument. He didn't want her wrecking his family—he'd already been broken by Tina moving away. He blamed Marilyn for that as well."

The stunning reality hit Rush. "He hit her with the crowbar."

Troy sadly nodded. "When he realized he'd killed her, he panicked and sent her car into the waters with Marilyn inside."

What was Marilyn doing at the lake in the first place? "The cuff link and mask we found in the car?"

"Dan's."

Too much of the mask had been unrecognizable, or Rush would have known earlier. "You let it go?" Rush hollered.

"I didn't even know for about a month. It ate him up until he had a breakdown and confessed it. By that time, she wasn't going to be found and no one was asking questions anymore." One shoulder lifted in an apologetic shrug. "I let it go to save my boy. I had to."

"You broke the law. You're an accomplice after the fact. He was seventeen. He could have been tried as a child, Troy, and you know it!"

"Marilyn ruined lives and probably had a criminal past—fleeing from some dangerous man. She was gone and people were glad. Even Joshua didn't do much to find her!"

Rush gaped at his mentor. "Are you saying Dan has

done all of this and you've been helping him?" He balled a fist.

"I haven't hurt anyone and I wasn't sure it was Dan at all until recently. He's been acting just like he did after he…after he did what he did."

What he did was second-degree murder.

"I don't want anybody else to get hurt."

A little late for that. "Where is Dan? Does he have Nora? And don't lie to me!"

"I don't know."

With Nora out of the way, and if Rush believed every word Troy said, Dan would have once again skated by with murder, and Troy would have once again been an accomplice after the fact. Without them discovering the truth about Gary Plenk, Troy would have never confessed.

He was thankful Nora hadn't given up.

"Where is Dan? I won't ask again."

"He's here at the party with Ainsley. Nora is safe."

"Nora hasn't been safe since she set out to discover the truth. And Hailey has been shot. Clearly, you're wrong. You and I will deal with this later, Troy. For now, find Joshua and tell him his daughter has been shot and is at the hospital. And if Dan's so much as laid one finger on Nora, I won't hesitate to put him in the ground and you too if you try to stop me." Rush flew from the house and jumped inside his Bronco. He'd deal with the hurt and betrayal later. At this moment, all he could think about was Nora and getting to her before it was too late.

"Dan, you want to talk. Let's talk." Nora backed toward the desk, hoping to get her cell and dial 911 while keeping Dan calm in the process. Fear zipped up her back, leaving a wake of chill bumps, but she found her clutch with her phone inside and slipped it into her hand. Dan didn't seem to notice. "What do you mean by asking why I dug into my mom's murder?"

Dan peeked out the door as if someone might be coming to interrupt him.

The power flickered again.

"Help me understand." Could Dan be involved? "Did you see my mom the night she died, Dan?" She crept toward the credenza by the door. If she could get to the door, she could bolt. Dan was unstable, unhinged. Warning bells rang in her head.

"I didn't mean to, Nora," he mumbled.

"You didn't mean to what?" Fear paralyzed her.

"I didn't mean to kill your mama. I just… I got so mad. I was in love with Tina and when her mom moved away with her, you know how hurt I was."

Dan admitted to murdering Mom. Nora's jaw dropped, but she recovered quickly. Anything to survive what might be about to happen. Admission meant he had no intention of letting her live. "I did know how hurt you were. I was so sorry about that. I liked Tina."

"It was your mom's fault, so when I saw my dad hugging her that night… I lost it. I mean… You can understand that, right?"

Troy did have an affair? He lied? "I can. Yes." She barely inched toward the door.

"I just wanted to talk to her. To tell her to leave my dad alone but she kept denying that they were involved. But I saw it with my own eyes! I grabbed the crowbar from the back of my truck and I…"

Nora didn't want to hear another word. Couldn't.

"I didn't mean it."

She took another small step.

"Where are you going?" Dan asked, and moved toward her. "You can't go anywhere, Nora. You can't leave this office. You don't understand."

The power flashed again and died.

Dan lunged.

Nora shrieked and grabbed a crystal paperweight on the credenza, bringing it down on Dan's head. He went limp and crumpled facedown on the floor. She only hoped he wasn't dead but knocked out. She wasn't planning on sticking around to find out, though. Once she found Rush, they could call an ambulance if it wasn't too late.

She tore from the office and into the hallway. "Lord, help me!" she whispered and kept running, tripping over her ball gown and boots.

She yelped as a figure appeared in front of her.

Dressed in a glittery midnight blue gown and matching mask, Ainsley Parkwell-Parsons stood with a gun in hand. "Where do you think you're going?"

Nora froze. "I— Ainsley, Dan—" Was she protecting Dan?

"Dan is an idiot," Ainsley said. "He's made one mistake after another. I'll deal with him. Right now, I'm going to deal with you."

"Rush knows!" Nora lied through her teeth hoping Ainsley would be too scared for whatever her intentions might be.

Ainsley gave her a look that stopped Nora in her tracks. "Rush might know Dan murdered your mother, maybe. And he might think that Dan's been coming after you to shut you up. Which means Rush only knows a half-truth. Give me that purse."

Blood whooshed in Nora's temples and her skin froze over, but she complied and tossed her clutch.

What was the half-truth?

"You make me sick. You have everything!" Ainsley used the gun to motion Nora back toward the offices. "The perfect life. Did you know that my dad owned this property before your precious savior of a father rescued him from debt and purchased it? I should be living on this mountain! I should have been the bright and shining star, not the girl always struggling financially."

"I—I didn't know."

"Of course not. You were too busy living a perfect life. With the perfect father. The perfect boyfriend. You should have never come back. I had what I wanted and you took him."

Rush? She wanted Rush? And a perfect life? Seriously?

"Where is Dan? I know he came after you. To warn you."

Warn her? Nora pointed toward Dad's office. "He's in there. He's...unconscious."

Ainsley forced her into the office. The sliver of moonlight only gave them a silhouette of Dan. He lay on the floor, blood surrounding his head, but he moved. He was alive! *Thank You, God!*

"He needs medical attention, Ainsley." Maybe she'd help her husband, forget Nora for a second and give her a chance to escape.

"No, he doesn't." She aimed the gun and fired, shooting Dan in the head.

Nora opened her mouth but a scream wouldn't leave her lips. Ainsley murdered her husband in cold blood, then she turned the gun on Nora. "Out the office exit. Now."

"You just killed your husband!" Nora held her hands up and walked on shaky legs toward the office exit that led up the steps and into the employee parking lot.

Ainsley forced her into the blizzard. Snow barreled down; the wind whipped against her dress. Ainsley didn't seem to be affected in her ball gown and ballet flats. Rage and homicide must be keeping her warm. Nora's teeth chattered.

"See that red car? Move."

"I don't understand," Nora said through trembling lips. "Why did you kill Dan? Why do you think I have a perfect life? Did you ever meet my mom?" The irony wasn't lost on Nora. "You have no idea how hard I've fought to not be the daughter of Marilyn Livingstone. You don't know how I feel. You only see what's on the outside and it's all been a lie, Ainsley. I'm not perfect. I'm an impostor." But she didn't want to be.

Ainsley pulled her keys from a hidden pocket on her evening gown and pressed a button. The trunk opened. "Get in. We're going for a ride."

"Where? Why? Rush is going to know that Dan didn't do this to me when they find him in the office. He's dead."

Ainsley's smile turned vile and malicious. "No, dear, he won't."

Nora looked down and gasped. Another body was already in the trunk. Dressed all in black. Nora recognized the coat and ski mask and build. "Who is this?" This man was the one who had repeatedly attacked Nora. "Dan didn't try to kill me?" Confusion wrapped around her brain, turning it foggy.

"No. Dan didn't try to kill you. He trusted his dad to keep things quiet and make this go away, and he would have if you hadn't shown up once again wrecking it all—wrecking my life. You had my childhood life. You had the man I wanted. And now you want to take my husband!"

"You just killed your husband!"

"I had to." Malicious eyes bore into Nora's. "You made him so crazy with your snooping, he went off the rails. Was going to confess to what he did all those years ago. I've learned if you want something, you have to take it. Make it happen. But when I started making things happen, he figured it out and he wanted to turn me in too!"

That's what Nora didn't understand according to Dan. He wasn't trying to kill her. Ainsley had been doing it all this time. He was there to rat her out and reveal his crime also. The guilt had been too much for him to bear.

Ainsley's long red hair whipped across her face, but she didn't shiver. "I'm about to make everything good that should have happened to me then, happen now."

Nora shook her head, confused. She stared at the man in her trunk. "Is this man...is he dead?"

"Do you see him breathing? Get in."

Ainsley wanted her to get in the trunk with a dead man. No.

"I can shoot you right here, Nora, but I find it poetic to make it happen where it all started. Where I found you in Rush's arms. You're no better than your mother. You don't deserve the perfect life you've been given. You don't deserve Rush. And when this is all over, when they discover that Dan hired this guy to kill you, he turned on Dan and killed him, then killed you, Rush will need comforting and so will I."

Ainsley. She hired this man to threaten Nora. Then to kill her when the threats wouldn't work. At first to help keep Dan's secret. But then... Revenge?

"You need a straitjacket not comfort!" Nora screeched. Her words were returned with a slap to her face.

"Get in!"

Nora slowly eased beside the corpse of the man who had once tried to murder her. "Who is he?"

"A brother of one of my students. Low-life drug dealer. No one special. But he botched the job mistaking your sister for you. Imagine my disappointment when I saw you alive and well heading for the stairwell." She put her hand on the trunk to close it. "So again. If you want something done, you do it yourself. Here I am."

She slammed the trunk shut and Nora heard the car start, then it moved. She could lie here and cry and remain confused or she could figure out how to stay alive. First off, she needed protection from the elements. The cold already worked through her bones, creating a stiffness in her joints. She rolled on her side, facing the dead man. Overcoming the fear of being next to him, she whispered an apology and rifled through his pockets.

Pocketknife. She took it and slid it down the top of her dress, then she removed his gloves and ski mask, his lifeless eyes staring back at her. She jerked and closed her eyes but used his ski mask as a hat and donned the leather gloves that had once wrapped around her throat.

Rush wouldn't let her out of his sight for long. Already, he had to be searching for her. Maybe he'd found Hailey, gotten her help. If she was actually alive. He'd find Dan dead and know someone had taken Nora when she was nowhere to be found.

Once they discovered this man, they'd connect the dots between Dan and him. No matter what scenario played out, no one would suspect Ainsley.

She'd be the grieving widow.

And Rush would be a grieving man. He'd feel guilty and responsible.

The horrifying truth smacked into her.

Nora's and Dan's deaths would bond Rush to Ainsley. Which was exactly what she wanted. To grieve together, comfort one another, form a new relationship—one she hoped would turn into a romance.

I've learned if you want something, you have to take it. Make it happen.

Rush would never suspect Ainsley. He'd dated her once. So there had to have been some kind of attraction there in the first place.

Tears filled Nora's eyes. Rush would always remember her leaving him. He'd always remember her back not her face.

God, help me. If I make it through this, help me change. Help me...help to run to You. Then give me the strength to go through the hard times, to hear the hard truths.

She had run. Away from God. From the people who loved her. Over and over. And all for what? So she could die alone in a blizzard because some crazy woman thought Nora had a perfect life. Perceptions were dangerous. She'd falsely perceived the way others thought of her and it had kept her insecure and hiding. There were so many things she wished she could go back and change, but it was too late.

Too late to tell Rush she'd made a dozen mistakes. If he were here now, she'd open up and tell him anything and everything he wanted to know. He was right about that too—two people had to communicate and be open and honest with one another.

She'd unlock everything she'd locked away after Mom died. She wouldn't bail. God would help her stay. Help her stick it out.

The car stopped.

The trunk opened and the barrel of the gun pointed at her head.

SIXTEEN

Rush blew through the main doors and into the ballroom. Candles illuminated the room. The band played and guests danced as if there wasn't a blizzard outside, and like the power wasn't totally out.

If Dan had hurt Nora…

He pushed his way through the crowd.

Gary Plenk.

Rush's fury burned hot. He'd deal with him soon enough. He asked locals if they'd seen Nora. Gary's wife spoke up. "I saw her going toward the stairwell earlier tonight. Dan Parsons was with her."

No.

"Thank you." He raced into the stairwell and hurtled down the stairs, then sprinted to Joshua's office.

Dan lay on the floor with a bullet wound to the back of the head.

Oh, no. Wait. Nora wasn't a killer and didn't have a gun. Someone else must have done this and taken Nora. But who?

Troy burst in behind him. "Joshua is at the hospital with Hailey. What can I do? I have to help do—" His sight landed on his son and he sank to his knees. "Dan! Oh, Dan!" He felt for a pulse but Rush knew what Troy surely deep down did. Dan was dead. If Dan wasn't the masked killer who had been attacking Nora, then someone else was in on it with him and somehow a struggle or something had taken place.

Troy continued repeating Dan's name.

Rush used Troy's radio on his shoulder and called it in, though it was far too late for an ambulance.

"I'm so sorry, Troy. Do you have any idea who might have done this?"

"No. Dan murdered Marilyn and he's been acting antsy lately. Especially the past couple of days. I had a hunch he was the one after Nora."

"But you never confirmed it with Dan?"

"No. He called me earlier this morning and told me he needed to talk to me, to tell me something. Get some advice. I assumed it was to confess what he'd been doing. I told him I'd take care of it and I thought I had. I guess he got scared."

"So who would do this? Because it wasn't Nora. Does anyone else know what Dan did all those years ago?" Gary was here; couldn't be him. Dan could have hired someone to do the dirty work and he killed Dan. But who? Was there anyone who might know anything? "Does Ainsley know?"

"Doubtful."

Dan was dressed in a tux, which meant he'd come to the party as a guest. "Troy." He laid a hand on his shoulder. "I'm sorry. I have to find Ainsley." She might know something Troy didn't.

"Go," he whispered. "I'm gonna stay here with my boy." His voice faltered. His sobs echoed through the quiet hall.

Inside the ballroom, throngs of people danced and milled around in masks. He had no time to waste. He went straight to the stage and took the microphone. He paged Ainsley but she didn't respond, didn't come forward. He left the stage. Who had Nora? Where would he have taken her?

Rush's heart pounded until it nearly beat out of his chest.

Gary Plenk approached. "I saw Ainsley earlier."

"You sure? Because we both know you're prone to lying." He glared until Gary had no way of denying that Rush now knew the truth.

Gary's face blanched. "I was backed into a corner, Rush. I made a mistake. I got back on the straight and narrow patch and haven't so much as looked at another woman. It would kill my wife to know."

"I don't care why you did you what you did. You're going to answer for lying about documents, but right now, tell me where you saw Ainsley."

"She was looking for Nora. My wife told her she was with Dan, like she told you. I haven't seen her since."

Maybe this crazed killer had Nora and Ainsley!

Or…

A more chilling thought grabbed him by the throat.

Could Ainsley be behind this? No. No way. But then he never imagined Dan would be a killer either. If Ainsley knew Dan was a killer, she'd have done whatever to help protect him. But who killed him?

"Rush." Troy ran toward him. "I found this outside the office." He held up a midnight blue mask with silver sequins. "It's Ainsley's. She drove separate tonight. I had two deputies check the lot for her car. It's not here."

Either the killer took them both hostage in Ainsley's car or Ainsley wasn't so innocent. "You think Ainsley has Nora? You think she killed Dan? Why?" Rush couldn't quite make the puzzle pieces fit.

"I know she didn't like Nora. Talked about her on occasion."

Then she hadn't put the past behind her.

If she took Nora, she couldn't have gotten far. Not with these weather conditions.

"Get everyone on the roads. We have to find them." *God, help us find her. Show us where to go.*

Ainsley stood over Nora, gun in hand. "I see you've warmed up. Don't you know dead bodies never stay that way? Out."

Nora climbed from the trunk of the car, her legs nearly numb from the weather. She glanced around. They were at Lookout Tower, which opened up to the Great Smoky Mountains. Any other day it would be breathtaking.

"You're going to shoot me? You can sleep at night knowing you're a murderer?"

"I'm counting on Rush's warm arms to keep me safe. I'll sleep like a baby."

"You're underestimating Rush. One, he will figure it out, and two, he was going to break up with you long before we had a thing. But go ahead and think otherwise—most delusionals do."

She was aggravating the situation, but if Ainsley thought Nora was going to roll over and go out without a fight—even a verbal one—she had another think coming.

Ainsley put the barrel of the gun to her head again. "I'd watch your mouth. Now, get him out of the trunk. You can do it. If I could get him in, you can get him out."

"Why?"

"Because he brought you here to kill you. You struggled. You shot him. But he got the gun before he died and he got you. You both died. It's tragic. Really."

Nora dragged the man to the lip of the trunk and struggled, but got him on the ground. As he landed something fell from his waistband.

A phone!

She bent to get a grip under his arms and snatched the phone. It was an older model. If she could find a way to call Rush without Ainsley noticing the light of the phone, he might be able to make it in time, and if not, he'd at least know she'd tried. The wind cracked a branch on a tree and Nora ducked as a limb fell.

Discreetly, she removed her right glove as she dragged him along the gravel. Tucking the phone in the folds of his heavy shirt, she dialed. Thankful his number was ridiculously easy. Sliding her thumb along the side of the phone, she turned the volume down so Ainsley wouldn't hear. The wind helped with noise control as it howled and whistled through the trees, bending them in odd angles. Any minute one might come down on them. Snow covered her hair, fell onto her eye lashes.

"Now what?" she asked and glanced down. Rush answered! "Why kill me at Lookout Tower, Ainsley? Shouldn't this be a reminder of what you lost? Don't you think Rush will figure out your plan?"

Hear me, Rush!

"Billy will take the fall for the murder. Are you a dunce, Nora? What am I thinking? You left a man like Rush not once, but twice, and if you weren't going to die tonight, third time's a charm. You're the dumbest woman I know."

"Billy. So that's the name of the man you hired to kill me. Well, at least I have a name to a dead face."

"Drop the body there."

Nora released the body to the ground in a way that kept the phone from being exposed.

This was the end. Rush wouldn't be able to get to her

in time. And she couldn't hear him if he was speaking on the other end of the line.

Headlights shone in the distance.

Ainsley whipped her head in that direction.

Nora pounced on the open opportunity and charged her, grabbing for the gun.

The lights came closer.

Nora struggled to get the gun, the wind not helping as it knocked her off balance. She and Ainsley fell to the snowy ground.

A car door slammed.

"Ainsley!" Rush called.

Ainsley turned.

"Run! Run, Nora!"

The gun went off, startling Nora. Then Ainsley kicked her and she slipped over the edge of the mountain, screaming.

Rush watched in horror as his future tumbled over the mountain, unsure if she'd been hit with a bullet. He raced to the edge. A splitting noise cracked through the night and before he could be sure what was happening a tree branch fell, knocking him down and his breath from his lungs, pinning him in the snow.

Nora! He had to get to Nora. To see if she was even alive. Moisture burned behind his eyes. What if she was lying down there bleeding out? Bones broken.

Legs. He couldn't feel his legs. Couldn't move anything but his arms. He pushed on the huge limb but it wasn't budging.

Nora had found a way to call him. He'd only been about five minutes from Lookout Tower when the call came.

He'd heard Nora loud and clear but she hadn't heard

him on the other end of the line. Hadn't heard his promise to come for her. To rescue her. That he loved her.

He hadn't rescued her. He hadn't been in time.

Rush fought and struggled but it was no use. He couldn't get the monstrous branch off his body.

"Hello, Rush."

Ainsley stood over him.

"Ainsley, help me."

"Why are you here?" She blinked as if they were chatting over lunch.

"Why do you think?"

Her eyes narrowed. "And that's why I won't help you. You're a liar and a cheater and the only reason you want out from under that tree is to see if you can save your precious Nora. Well, guess what? You can't. She's lying down there dead as a rock. But don't worry, you'll meet her soon."

"And what exactly will you tell Troy?" His gun was out of reach. If he could get her closer he might be able to get a hold on her, choke her out, but that didn't help him out from under the tree.

"That Billy Arnold kidnapped me and Nora. Killed Nora, shot me. I'll have to shoot my leg or something, I guess. You showed up and this tree fell on you and he shot you too. I'm the lone survivor. For once I'll be in the spotlight and beloved by all and not Nora. High time."

Rush didn't have the fight to tell her how many plot holes were in that story. Troy wasn't stupid, just blinded by love for his son. He'd sniff the truth out before Ainsley realized she'd have gun powder residue on her hands.

"I loved you, Rush. I've loved you since seventh grade when you climbed a tree to rescue my cat. Kinda fitting a tree is between us now. Did you ever love me?"

Rush closed his eyes. Here came the kill shot. Because he wasn't going to lie. He couldn't.

Nora's lungs burned and she was pretty sure she'd broken more than one rib. Her entire body convulsed in pain. She tasted blood in her mouth but she was alive and bullet-free. Ainsley had missed. But she thought she'd heard another gun go off.

Which meant Rush might be dead, but Nora wasn't going to lie here and do nothing. She wasn't going to burrow into the snow and let it rob her of her life. She wouldn't cut loose now. Army crawling toward the side of the mountain, she gripped a tree branch and pulled herself up, clawing and struggling to make it to the top.

Soaked hair, clothes and feet, her fingers and toes numb, she kept fighting to reach Rush. She'd take a bullet, a knife, being mowed over by a car even; it didn't matter. All she could think about was falling into his arms.

Dead or alive.

God, let him be alive.

She had skidded and slipped down the mountain, losing a boot and ripping her dress, her skin frostbit and everything that wasn't numb ached, but she forged ahead until she made it to the top.

Ainsley stood over Rush.

A tree! He was pinned down.

Wind howled. Trees swayed until they nearly touched the ground. She hunted for something. Found a large piece of wood and snatched it up as she fought for every step; every breath felt like knives stabbing her as she inched closer and closer to Ainsley. But she would not leave even if he'd begged her to go. She'd die fighting for Rush. For them.

For love.

* * *

"No, Ainsley. I'm sorry," Rush said. "I've always loved Nora. It's always been her. It will always be her." It didn't take much light to see the fire in Ainsley's eyes at his rejection. At his truth. Maybe he should have lied. But Ainsley would have seen that too.

A shadow behind Ainsley caught his eye.

"I hoped your answer would be different."

She aimed.

The shadow from behind raised its arm and brought something down hard on Ainsley's head. She toppled into the snow, unmoving.

"Rush!" Nora cried, and fell to her knees beside him.

"Nora?" She was alive. She was the shadow. "How? Wait…get the gun, Nora Beth."

She scurried through the snow and grabbed Ainsley's gun. "Tell me what to do, Rush." She studied the tree. "I don't know if I can move it. But I'll try."

This woman had climbed half a mountain bloodied and broken for him. Instead of making herself scarce like he'd told her to, she'd saved him. On her own.

"Get my radio. It fell." She felt under his legs until she found it lodged in the snow. She gave him the radio and he called it in. Nora ran her hands through his wet hair. "Go get in the car, Nora Beth. Turn it on and try to get warm."

"No," she protested.

"Nora, you're injured. It's freezing. Go get in the car."

"No!" She stroked his cheek. "I'm not leaving you again. No matter what. Understand? I'm. Not. Leaving."

"Not even for Florida?" he asked and tried to smile, but even that hurt.

"Not even for Florida. I want to stay. If you can forgive me. If you love me enough to try one last time." She sniffed. "Because I love you. I don't want to keep secrets or hide things away. And I don't want to run. Not anymore. Not even to your car. I'm done running from everything. From you, especially."

He grabbed her hand and kissed it. "I love you, Nora Beth. Don't go to Florida. Stay here. With me. For always."

Sirens wailed.

"For always."

"Nora Beth?"

"Yeah," she whispered, and tottered.

"Merry Christmas, love."

"Merry Christmas," she said, and collapsed in the snow.

SEVENTEEN

Nora stood in Dad's kitchen. Tomorrow was New Year's Eve and Nora was thankful that in this new year she would live and so would Rush and Hailey.

Hailey had emergency surgery, spent several days in the hospital, but she was home now, resting in bed. Nora carried a cup of tea to her, limping with the lovely black boot she was stuck with for a while. They'd taped up her ribs, given her pain meds and diagnosed her with a mild concussion. But she'd made it.

So had Rush. Broken leg. Bruised femur. But alive and recovering.

Nora knocked on her sister's bedroom door.

"Come in."

She opened the door. Hailey lay in bed, pale but smiling. Nathan sat next to her. He kissed her forehead and scooted off the bed. "I'm going to check on Dalton. Make sure he's not sitting in cold bathwater. Him and his boats." He patted Nora's shoulder and left.

"I brought you tea."

"Thanks."

"I'm sorry," Nora said.

"You say that every time you look at me. Stop. It's over, and the truth is that while I'm not thanking God I got shot and almost died, I am thanking Him for causing some good to come from it. Nathan has been by my side since I woke up from surgery. It was a wake-up call for us, and we're going to work things out. We love each other, Nora. I'm not sure we would have let ourselves feel that again had I not almost been gone for good. So stop the sorry bit. Okay?"

She handed Hailey her tea and squeezed her hand. "Okay."

"Nathan told me that Gary Plenk admitted his affair to his wife. She left him. I hope they can work it out."

"I do too."

"And the money in Mom's trunk. Will you be okay not knowing why it was there, Nora?"

Nora sighed. "I've had to learn the hard way that not every question comes with an answer. Some things we have to carry through life not knowing, but trusting that God does and He's got it. Was she blackmailed? Was she taking it to vanish? To abandon us? I don't know. I have to find peace there. We all do. And even if that was what was happening, I know God never leaves us. Never abandons us. He loves us so much. I'm going to rest in that knowledge. Find who I am in the light of who Jesus is. I've never attempted that before."

Hailey snickered and moaned. "What about Billy Arnold?"

"His parents have been notified of his death and that he was being blackmailed by Ainsley. Everyone is grieving in one way or another. But it's a new season. A New Year is upon us."

"And you're staying."

"I am." She'd confessed her debts to Dad and he'd canceled them. Paid it all for her. No strings attached. Nothing but grace. "I think I'm going to do some private meteorology work. For mountain climbers, et cetera, and I'll keep up the forensic meteorology. Dad said I can stay in the chalet as long as I'd like."

"And Rush?" Hailey asked.

"Rush and I haven't talked turkey yet." She laughed. "We love each other. So far that's enough. I didn't used to think so." She stood.

"What changed?"

"I learned that love truly does cover a multitude of sins—not condones but covers. It can cover faults, flaws and mistakes. God's love. And if His love can do that and He can continually stick with us, then His love can do that through His people to one another." Nora blew Hailey a kiss. "Get some rest."

"Ditto."

Nora left and entered the living room. Rush stood by the hearth. "You feel like a sleigh ride?" He motioned with his chin to the front door. Nora spotted a sleigh outside.

"If you're going. I'll go anywhere with you."

His eyes lit up and he hobbled over. "We're peas in a pod, aren't we?"

"We're something." She grabbed her coat and they managed to get outside and into the sleigh, laughing at their injuries and lack of grace.

Rush covered them with a blanket and took her hand. "Troy's going to have to go to prison, Nora. I know what he did was wrong, but it kills me."

She leaned on his shoulder. "I'm sorry, Rush. What's that mean for you and the department?"

"I'm going to be interim sheriff until it's time to run in the fall."

"You'll make a great sheriff."

He shifted and looked deep into her eyes, stirring an

old longing and dream in her heart. "You think I'll make a great husband?"

She swallowed as he reached into his pocket.

"I think you'll make the greatest husband. And father."

He raised an eyebrow playfully. "Oh, yeah?"

"Yeah."

"Nora Beth, I've loved you my whole life. I want to finish it out loving you. Would you marry me?" He opened a velvety box to reveal a round solitaire diamond with small diamonds on each side.

Nora gasped at the beauty of the ring, but more so at the love Rush had for her and the journey it had taken to bring them to this point. "It's all I've ever wanted, Rush. Yes."

He placed the ring on her finger, kissed her knuckle, then framed her face. "You're all I'll ever want." He claimed her lips, gingerly, then more possessive. Pouring into her promise and hope. Like a guarantee of their future together. No running away. Only to each other and to God.

He nuzzled her nose. "I was thinking a Christmas wedding."

"I don't want to wait one more year, Rush. I don't even want to wait another day."

Laughing, he kissed her nose and cheeks. "What I meant to say was, I was thinking of a New Year's Eve wedding. Me, you, our family outside under the pines and my dad officiating. If we can get a license that fast."

"It's Tennessee. Got a valid picture ID?" She laughed. A few poinsettias around the glorious snow. Family surrounding them. "It's how I want to start the new year, Rush. Married to you. I don't care if we're in boots and bruised. We can have a reception at the lodge in a few weeks and take pictures then. I just want to be your wife. Finally."

"I can't think of anything I want more. I've been praying for this day. Can't say I loved the waiting period, but it was worth it. So worth it."

He gazed into her eyes. The love shining in them reached deep into her soul, warming it like a cozy fire. Life wouldn't always be sunny skies and warm breezes. Storm clouds would roll in. Cold fronts. Maybe even hailstorms.

But Nora would remember when storms came. When the cold crept up, she had a place to run for shelter. In the arms of God.

And into Rush's arms.

For always.

* * * * *

Don't miss these other Love Inspired Suspense books by Jessica R. Patch:

Fatal Reunion
Protective Duty
Concealed Identity
Final Verdict
Deep Waters
Secret Service Setup
Dangerous Obsession

Available now from Love Inspired Suspense!

Find more great reads at www.Harlequin.com.

Dear Reader,

When I think about Jesus, I think about how He was born into scandal. How many people believed that a young girl who was betrothed to another man really was carrying the Son of God? I'm sure there were whispers all His life about how His mother must have "stepped out" on Joseph. Yet Joseph married her anyway—thanks to a dream from God. He loved her amidst the rumors. I wanted to write about that.

Nora was born into scandal. She lived in that shadow for so long. Rumors. But not only did Joshua—her adopted father—love her as his own, God loved her as His very own. God loves you. You are His very own. No matter what your background, what you were born into or what happened to you that you had no control over. You can come out from under that shadow and live in the light through the sweet, healing love of Jesus. You can be free to be who you are meant to be in Christ.

I love to hear from readers. Please email me at: jessica @jessicarpatch.com and visit my website at www.jessica rpatch.com. Don't forget to sign up for my newsletter, *Patched In*, to receive book news, sales and freebies while you're there!

Merry Christmas,
Jessica

SPECIAL EXCERPT FROM

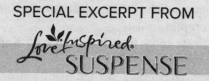

Love Inspired.
SUSPENSE

*With a price on his witness's head,
US marshal Jonathan Mast can think of only
one place to hide Celeste Alexander—in the
Amish community he left behind. But will this trip
home save their lives…and convince them that a
Plain life together is worth fighting for?*

*Read on for a sneak preview of
Amish Hideout by Maggie K. Black,
the exciting beginning to the Amish Witness Protection
miniseries, available January 2019
from Love Inspired Suspense!*

Time was running out for Celeste Alexander. Her fingers flew over the keyboard, knowing each keystroke could be her last before US marshal Jonathan Mast arrived to escort her to her new life in the witness protection program.

"You gave her a laptop?" US marshal Stacy Preston demanded. "Please tell me you didn't let her go online."

"Of course not! She had a basic tablet, with the internet capability disabled." US marshal Karl Adams shot back even before Stacy had finished her sentence.

The battery died. She groaned. Well, that was that.

"You guys mind if I go upstairs and get my charging cable?"

The room went black. Then she heard the distant sound of gunfire erupting outside.

"Get Celeste away from the windows!" Karl shouted. "I'll cover the front."

What was happening? She felt Stacy's strong hand on her arm pulling her out of her chair.

"Come on!" Stacy shouted. "We have to hurry—"

Her voice was swallowed up in the sound of an explosion, expanding and roaring around them, shattering the windows, tossing Celeste backward and engulfing the living room in smoke. Celeste hit the floor, rolled and hit a door frame. She crawled through it, trying to get away from the smoke billowing behind her.

Suddenly a strong hand grabbed her out of the darkness, taking her by the arm and pulling her up to her feet so sharply she stumbled backward into a small room. The door closed behind them. She opened her mouth to scream, but a second hand clamped over her mouth. A flashlight flickered on and she looked up through the smoky haze, past worn blue jeans and a leather jacket, to see the strong lines of a firm jaw trimmed with a black beard, a straight nose and serious eyes staring into hers.

"Celeste Alexander?" He flashed a badge. "I'm Marshal Jonathan Mast. Stay close. I'll keep you safe."

Don't miss
Amish Hideout by Maggie K. Black,
available January 2019 wherever
Love Inspired® Suspense books and ebooks are sold.

www.LoveInspired.com